JUSTICE

A Play

Dyanna Morrison

ISBN: 978-1-7359116-1-8

With Gratitude

I have to express deep gratitude to my Dad and Mom, Annie and Uncle for everything you did for me during our years together. I miss you all so much! Thank you for a lifetime of love and support!

To my dear friends, Cheryl and Mike, for your friendship, suggestions, sunny sailing days and technical expertise. I couldn't have pulled this all together without your help!

Many thanks to RL Sather for the cover/art work!

Lastly, to my dear Uncle Norm, for putting this story in my head during our Thursday lunch dates, that I could never quite walk away from. I know that you are somewhere above the clouds, having a "tuni" in the sky and watching over me. I promised you one day I would write you a story. I kept my promise!

Contents

FOREWORD

Before you read my play, *Justice*, it seemed like a good idea to explain what this play is not intended to be, prior to explaining my intentions for what it is supposed to be. *Justice* is not intended to be a white woman's tone deaf response to the current Black Lives Matter movement. I've been working on this trilogy for over nineteen years. Throughout this time, it has become clear to me that many are either unaware or don't recall all of the prevailing circumstances of those times, that influenced the founding doctrines and documents. Slavery was, is, and always will be, woefully wrong and an everlasting stain on the founding and early history of our country. Our founding fathers knew slavery was wrong and incongruous with our founding principles of, "Liberty and Justice for all."

In acknowledging the shortcomings of The Articles of Confederation, the framers galvanized and mobilized, to pen more comprehensive documents that would become our Constitution and The Bill of Rights, serving to unite our country. In 1784, when Thomas Jefferson's proposal to ban slavery from the trans-Appalachian West failed by one vote, he lamented, "And Heaven was silent in that awful moment." From inception, the two major areas of disagreement were slavery and who will have the power to control it and the separation of powers between the states and national government. By the time of the Constitutional Convention in 1787, many states had already abolished slavery, including: Vermont, Pennsylvania, Massachusetts, New Hampshire, Connecticut and Rhode Island. The Northwest Ordinance of 1787 forever banned slavery in the states we now know as Ohio, Indiana, Michigan, Illinois, Wisconsin and part of Minnesota. 90% of slaves lived in the South.

The southern states were already threatening succession during the debates to get our Constitution and The Bill of Rights ratified. This young country could not withstand another bloody and costly battle and was still recovering from the years of our fight for freedom from King George III and England. Accordingly, the framers incorporated Section

1, Article 9, into the Constitution, which barred Congress from banning the importation of slaves before 1808, with all intentions that the future generation would carry through on the gradual phasing out of slavery, which meanwhile, would allow our country to gain strength and realize a financial recovery from the aftermath of the revolution. The Three-Fifths Compromise provided an incentive for states to continue the emancipation process. When a state freed its slaves, it would get increased representation in the House of Representatives. This became known as the "federal ratio," and Alexander Hamilton later concurred that without the federal ratio, "no union could have possibly been formed." The Fugitive Slave Clause created considerable angst among the majority of framers, but they again conceded to ensure ratification. Considering all of the obstacles that were present, the rancorous debate that ensued, and the level of compromise needed on both sides of the issues, George Washington viewed the ratification of these penultimate documents as, "little short of a miracle." One of our founder's greatest miscalculations was in assuming that the future generation (s) would be as enlightened and receptive to the art of compromise as they had been, and clearly, this was not the case.

Our framers knew that slavery was wrong and referred to it as "their odious bargain with sin." In his "Notes on the State of Virginia," Thomas Jefferson said, "I tremble for my Country when I reflect that God is just; that his justice cannot sleep forever." He was referring to slavery and much of the dialogues spoken in Act II, Scene 4, are their words. Our first President, George Washington, favored Alexander Hamilton's proposal of a national bank versus Thomas Jefferson's agrarian–based economy, because farming and agriculture relied heavily on slavery, whereas a commercial model did not. He once told a visitor to Mount Vernon, "I clearly foresee, that nothing but the rooting out of slavery can perpetuate the existence of our Union," as directly quoted in Act II, Scene 4.

In 1806, now President Jefferson, in his annual message to Congress, "Congratulated," his fellow citizens as the year of 1808 neared, when they could finally legislate against slavery. He encouraged them to act with a sense of urgency, passing a law to go into effect, Jan 1, 1808. Jefferson's vision was, "to withdraw the Citizens of the U.S. from all further participation in those violations of human rights which have been so long continued on the unoffending inhabitants of Africa, and which the morality, the reputation, and the best interests of our country have long been eager to proscribe." In later years, The Missouri Compromise fueled Jefferson's concerns. The invention of the Cotton Gin was a boon to the slave trade, as cotton grew to be the sweetheart crop of the South. Slavery flourished versus contracting, causing Jefferson, in retirement, to further state, "This momentous question, like a fire bell in the night, awakened and filled me with terror. I considered it the knell of the union. We have the wolf by the ear, and we can neither hold him, nor safely let him go. Justice is in one scale, and self-preservation in the other. "

Former slave/abolitionist, Frederick Douglass, spoke realistically of our founders and founding documents, stating the following, "Now take the Constitution according to its plain reading, and I defy the presentation of a single pro slavery clause in it. On the other hand, it will be found to contain principles and purposes entirely hostile to the existence of slavery." In 1852 at an Independence Day celebration in Rochester, NY, he further stated that our founders, "Were brave men. They were great men, too, great enough to give fame to a great age, for the good they did, and the principles they contended for, I will unite with you to honor their memory." Yet, in another speech in 1852, Douglass, also recognized the framer's dualities, and was also quoted as saying, "What, to the American slave, is your 4th of July? I answer: a day that reveals to him, more than all other days in the year, the gross injustice and cruelty to which he is the constant victim. To him, your celebration is a sham; your boasted liberty, an unholy license; your national greatness, swelling vanity." He understood both the inherent complexities of the state of our union at that time, and the hypocrisies. The legal framework that shaped our democracy has allowed us to remain the oldest enduring republic in history.

Unfortunately, the issues surrounding slavery kept getting thrust to the future. The Compromise of 1850, The Kansas Nebraska Act of 1854 and the 1857 Supreme Court decision in the Dred Scott case all continued to have devastating consequences for the anti-slavery movement. Abolitionist candidate, Abraham Lincoln, frequently referenced our founding documents as justification for emancipation. In 1861, the election of anti-slavery candidate Abraham Lincoln to the office of President was a turning point, and by the time he was getting ready to be sworn into office, seven states had already seceded from the Union. This inevitably resulted in the devastating loss of over 618,000 men in The Civil War, which was the antithesis of democracy, serving to expose longstanding racist sentiments amongst the Southern states and other areas of the union, which unfortunately remains the prevailing sentiment for far too many, to this day. Lincoln's Emancipation Proclamation was signed into law in 1863 and the Thirteenth Amendment was passed in 1865, which abolished slavery. In 1868, the Fourteenth Amendment gave black citizens equal protection under the law. The Fifteenth Amendment was passed in 1870, giving black citizens the right to vote. In 1896 the U.S. Supreme Court ruling in Plessy V. Ferguson upheld the, "separate but equal," finding for racial segregation in public places and it was not until the Civil Rights movement that began in the 1950s and 1960s that additional legislation was passed in both the Civil Rights Act of 1957 and the Civil Rights Act of 1964, providing hollow, but further measures for integration and equality.

I support tearing down confederate monuments and renaming military bases, because confederate leaders represented a backward thinking ideology, nearly one hundred years after our founding, resulting in the Civil War, which was always about slavery. Our Southern states/leaders wanted to end our union and perpetuate slavery. Conversely, our founders fought for our freedom and then fought for our unification. We are a country of great freedoms that are the envy of many nations and our founders deserve recognition for that. The issues surrounding slavery are central to our founding and should be taught side by side in our classrooms, allowing us to recognize our founder's accomplishments, while addressing their shortfalls.

Would *Hamilton* be as successful if it were released today versus 2015? It has every reason to be, because of its portrayal of American history through a unique lens. In a recent article, Lin Manuel Miranda, was quoted as saying that the founding fathers did not address slavery in the Constitution, but as referenced above, they did. There continues to be a subset of viewers who were or are critical of *Hamilton* on account of its failure to highlight the issue of slavery. Playwright, Ishmael Reed, aired these viewpoints in his work, "The Haunting of Lin-Manuel Miranda."

There was even a recent flood of cries on the internet to cancel *Hamilton*, after its recent Disney release. *Hamilton*, should be remembered for its theatrical, uplifting portrayal of our founders/founding and the music that will live on in our hearts for years to come, shining a spotlight on many of the positive interactions and outcomes during the infancy of our country, which I have been trying to do for a very long time. So, it was important to me in this current edit of 2017-2018, to highlight and discuss the founder's views on slavery. I corresponded with LMM on July 30, 2018, to share my ongoing efforts for recognition/production of *Justice*, which included the Charlottesville flashback scene. He was gracious enough to send me a personal handwritten response in September 2018, encouraging me, "to keep producing such important work."

In July 2020, FOX News reported on a poll that they conducted, which revealed: 63% of Americans viewed the founders as heroes; 15% viewed them as villains; 15% said it depends and the remaining 7% had no opinion one way or the other. They were patriots and they were a group of men with a vision for a free nation of self-governance, set out to establish a republic, with a scope that had never been done before and most thought could not be accomplished. Our "experiment" with democracy continues, as we strive to create a more perfect union.

In July 2020, NBC News THINK, conducted a poll asking Americans how satisfied they were with our democracy and thoughts on changes to the U.S. system of governing and elections, broken down by age, race, income and education across the country. The first question asked was, "Overall, how satisfied are you with the way democracy works in the United States, with answers ranging from not at all satisfied to very satisfied. "Fairly satisfied," was the most selected answer at 42%. The polling data further explained that the level of dissatisfaction in the U.S. has nearly doubled since 1995, but I think the key point to take away here is that, "One can be dissatisfied with the way that democracy is working but still be committed to democracy. In fact, that may be the ultimate test of commitment to a system that sometimes puts power in leaders with whom you disagree." I eagerly await the November 3, 2020 election, where I will exercise my right to vote my conscience, because that is how change is brought about in a democracy.

Also, in August 2020, NBC News THINK, published an opinion/article, about George Mason University, named for a slave-owning founding father, and shared the thoughts of this University's first black President, Dr. Gregory Washington. Dr. Washington was immediately asked by a reporter, "Should George Mason University's name change?" His response was, "The question is a legitimate one – and it's worth considering." Dr. Washington goes on to posit, "Should we then now continue to recognize George Mason and other founders as brilliant and devoted patriots? Or should we condemn them for ignoring the basic ideals by which they defined this country? We should do both, because Mason is the very embodiment of the duality of America, which we celebrate for its insistence on liberty and justice for all, even though it enslaved and segregated millions of its own people for most of its history.... We can neither run away from the atrocities committed throughout this nation's history, nor from the fact that the core principles established by founders like Mason – like fairness, equality and liberty – were also the foundational principles employed by the civil rights and other movements."

Justice is meant to be an inspirational, historical drama, using two contemporary court cases involving First Amendment protection/abuses and provides thoughtful reflection about what the guys who wrote the stuff, might think if they had the opportunity to witness these proceedings. What would they think if they could actually see how the Constitution and The Bill of Rights that they penned over two hundred and forty years ago was being applied in contemporary legal proceedings and would they agree? Based on more than nineteen years of research, much of the words the founders speak, are actually their words, verbatim. I came very close to getting the original version of *Justice* produced at a theater in northern California for the 2006 season and most recently met with a local theater in Rhode Island, who had given *Justice,* the nod to open its new play series in November of 2020 but then the Corona Virus pandemic hit, and as they say, timing is everything.

The first trial revolves around the actual arrests of over two hundred protesters, in Washington, D.C., during the Inauguration Day ceremonies of Donald Trump on January 20, 2017, now commonly referred to as the "J20" trials. The Department of Justice was allowed to wrongfully charge over two hundred protesters with crimes that could have resulted in over 60 years in prison. These arrests were the catalyst that compelled me to do a major rewrite of the script in 2017/18. I remain surprised at the lack of awareness surrounding these proceedings and that most people today are unaware of these arrests and the resulting trials that proved to be largely unsuccessful for the Department of Justice. The first six protesters being tried were acquitted of all charges and the charges against the remaining 180+ protesters eventually were dropped. Though these proceedings did receive media coverage, these arrests largely flew under the radar and merited far more outrage than they received. These charges were clear violations of these protesters First Amendment rights and the most recent events of police brutality, using tear gas and excessive force to remove peaceful protesters from Lafayette Square on June 1, 2020, and the July 2020 deployment of Federal forces to Portland, should come as no surprise. Thankfully, the majority of the protests resulting from the very public asphyxiation of George Floyd, which helped to rightly reignite the Black Lives Matter movement, have been largely peaceful and have been allowed to persist and expand because of the First Amendment rights laid down for us in our Bill of Rights. Many other countries do not enjoy these basic rights. The conversations that we are now having regarding systemic racism and police brutality are long overdue and I hope that they will continue to result in passing meaningful local, state and national legislation. We have been down this road too many times before but, this time, it does seem like there has been an unprecedented recognition that racial inequality and injustice are still very much a part of our societal footprint and can no longer be ignored or tolerated.

The second trial is loosely based on the events at the Charlottesville "Unite the Right" rally that occurred on August 11-12, 2017, culminating in the largest public gathering of white supremacists in our country in years. At the time of beginning the rewrite, I upped the charges to criminal, versus the civil charges initially filed, to heighten the suspense and because it didn't seem that unrealistic based on the preponderance of actual, documented evidence surrounding the premeditated violence, injuries and death that resulted. Initially the only criminal charges that were filed were against the driver of the vehicle that killed Heather Heyer. In July 2018 the Department of Justice allowed other lawsuits to move forward charging dozens of white supremacists with the intention of committing violence and have resulted in successful convictions. So, the script correctly anticipated these charges a year in advance of the actual filings.

The poignant flashback scene between George Washington and Benjamin Franklin is meant to be a welcome and timely reminder of the multitude of contributions this sage and great man made to our young country. I had personally forgotten or was unaware of many of the significant accomplishments Franklin realized during his lifetime, until I started doing the research for this script back in the early 2000s. Once a slave owner, his view on slavery drastically changed over the course of years, resulting in his freeing his own slaves and introducing a petition to Congress in 1790 on behalf of the Pennsylvania Society for Promoting the Abolition of Slavery, as factually highlighted on page 63. A brilliant inventor and a great mind, who had no more than a grade school education, earned honorary degrees from The College of William and Mary in 1756 and doctorates from the University of St. Andrews in 1759 and the University of Oxford in 1762 for his scientific accomplishments. I have great respect for all of his contributions.

The doctrines of white supremacy are not only racist, but anti-Semitic and homophobic. My intention was for Judge Porter's sentencing to emphatically denounce all of these outdated ideologies and end in a hope-filled message of patriotism.

It is my hope, that after reading *Justice*, readers will take away the exact intent of my message: that our First Amendment rights, specifically, Freedom of Speech, Freedom of the Press and the Right to Peaceably Gather/Protest, are critical to our founding principles and rights as Americans, and they are currently being threatened; that any type of systemic racism, oppression, hate crime, domestic terrorism, discrimination or intolerance is wrong and are contradictions to what we, as Americans stand for; that our founders, though flawed and imperfect, still managed to institute a Democratic Republic that remains intact in the year of 2020. Their fierce ideological debates and collaboration, led to consensus, culminating in an unprecedented legal framework of self-government that has stood the test of time, and though our systems of checks and balances are currently being tested, we need to remain confident that justice will prevail in our country, that our democracy will once again flourish, and that permanent changes will be made to recognize and right the wrongs of injustice and intolerance for good. These are difficult times and important conversations that we are having. As Abraham Lincoln so aptly stated, "We simply must begin with and mold from disorganized and discordant elements."

Our country and our laws are far from perfect, but I will remain optimistic that better days are ahead, and I will still appreciate the many things our founders and our country got right. Tearing down our founding fathers' statutes doesn't seem like the right course of action. I choose to look at the plurality of their contributions, versus making a binary judgment, because it seems reasonable and fair. We wouldn't have our Constitution, our Bill of Rights, or our democracy without them. There are always two ways of looking at every situation and I respect the opinions of those who think differently.

I will continue to uphold that if it weren't for the political astuteness of our founders that many of the basic rights that we take for granted as American citizens might not be our reality today. It doesn't mean that I don't denounce slavery, systemic racism, police brutality or oppression of every kind! I think that we, as a country, can move forward more effectively together versus apart. Our founders sought to create a country more in line with their ideologies and created a Constitution/Bill of Rights that was meant to be a, "living document." In *Federalist* 14, James Madison, discusses the future and the experience of the people of America, in saying, "...They pursued a new and more noble course. They accomplished a revolution which has no parallel in the annals of human society. They reared the fabrics of governments which have no model on the face of the globe. They formed the design of a great Confederacy, **which it is incumbent on their successors to improve and perpetuate**." I think that sums it up well. Instead of singularly focusing on judging our founders through a contemporary lens, two hundred and forty years later, we should also be giving equal scrutiny to other administrations between now and then, who with a few exceptions, including, Abraham Lincoln, JFK, LBJ and Obama, collectively continued to ignore, perpetuate and/or accelerate the issues of social and racial injustice, culminating in the national day of reckoning that is now rightly upon us. We have the ability and the responsibility to shape our future, but we, the people, cannot do it alone. We must call upon the leadership of all three branches of our government; the Executive, Judicial, and Legislative, to lead these efforts, unencumbered by partisan politics. Together, we have the power to make or break our democracy! Democracy wasn't a yes or no question back in the days of our founding and it is not a yes or no answer today in the year of 2020. Democracy requires debate and disagreement and ultimately, compromise.

Characters

Bailiff

Foreperson/Jurors

Reporter

Judge Grace Porter

Gabrielle Porter

Mitchell Haverhill

Helen Hutchings

Michael Pantovere

Leonard Snayder

Noah Lester

A.J.

Spencer Matthew

Tyrone Walker

George Washington

Benjamin Franklin

John Adams

Alexander Hamilton

Thomas Jefferson

James Madison

ACT I

CONFLICT

I.1 INT. Mitch's house - EVENING

> *Grace Porter, a tall,*
> *statuesque, beautiful brunette*
> *is in the kitchen making tea.*
> *Mitchell Haverhill, her tall,*
> *handsome boyfriend is in the*
> *living room.*
>
> *She is wearing one of Mitch's*
> *oversized dress shirts and he*
> *is running around in his*
> *boxers.*

                    GRACE

          (Yelling over her shoulder to
            Mitch)

Hey Mitch! Did you happen to see the local news
last night?

                    MITCH

No, why?

                    GRACE

One of the reporters was doing the out on the
town question thing, which started out as a
commemoration of Veteran's Day and then morphed

into this patriotic conversation about the
founding of our country and the framers. So,
the conversations unfolded from there and at
least two of the three people he stopped, didn't
know who the first President of the United
States was!

                    MITCH

NO!

                    GRACE

YES!

                    MITCH

And don't tell me...

          (pauses)

They also thought that John Adams was a beer!

          (laughing)

                    GRACE

I think he was afraid to go any farther after
that one!

          (laughing)

                         *She brings two mugs of tea
                         into the living room and she
                         and Mitch curl up on the
                         couch.*

MITCH

What's on your docket for tomorrow?

GRACE

We're expecting the jury to come back with the verdicts for the first group of protesters charged as a result of the Inauguration Day Protester arrests, on January 20, 2017, which are now commonly referred to as "J20."

MITCH

So how do you like presiding over this case in Superior Court so far?

GRACE

Well, so far, it's been equal parts of interesting and disturbing

MITCH

And the disturbing part is that these protesters, who were in fact simply exercising their First Amendment rights, have now been slapped with felony rioting charges, despite the fact there is no proof that any of them actually inflicted any damage the day of the Inauguration.

GRACE

Exactly! I am concerned that this new administration is trying to send a message to anyone that stands up in defiance. I already issued a judgment of acquittal on a felony count of inciting a riot because the evidence just wouldn't support it. That still leaves two misdemeanor rioting charges and five felonies in connection with property destruction. They charged over two hundred protesters. This is just the first six.

                    MITCH

I defer to your legal expertise, but it seems that these charges, even after being reduced, seem all too encompassing and overreaching.

                    GRACE

Ugh, right. I fear it is nothing more than a very public and very costly power play. The legal process can be all too intimidating. Some of these defendants have had to quit their jobs and temporarily relocate here to satisfy all of the prosecutorial demands, when at first glance, the majority of them seem to have only been exercising their rights to protest, to peaceful assembly.

                    MITCH

Well your liberal boyfriend is grateful for the "Blue Wave" as a result of November's elections!

                    GRACE

Let's not have this conversation right now!

                    MITCH

Why not?

                    GRACE

Because your conservative girlfriend doesn't
want to have an argument

                    MITCH

Let's have this conversation. Your opinion is
always "illuminating," conservative but
"illuminating."

                    GRACE

Oh oh, here we go. OK, freedom of speech does
not mean anarchy, Mitch. I went to Law school,
you went to Med school. I agree with you that
the Prosecutor's charges seem broadly-based and
overreaching, but if the jury comes back with a
guilty verdict, they will have performed their
duties responsibly.

                    MITCH

Grace, just because your father was one of the
most conservative Supreme Court Justices in
history to ever preside and I say that with all
due respect, doesn't mean you have to follow
suit. Standing up for your own convictions will
not mean you're letting your father down or
minimizing his legacy.

                    GRACE

You think all of this has something to do with
fearing my Father's disapproval? My dead
Father's disapproval?

            (now totally and visibly upset)

How's about we forgo your Freudian psychobabble
and just admit that sometimes it's as simple as
black and white. The written word of the law.

                    MITCH

Freudian psychobabble?

            (equally agitated)

                    GRACE

I've had enough of this conversation! I'm going
to bed.

            (pauses and speaks angrily)

I hope you won't mind sleeping with such a
dysfunctional overachiever, who is
subconsciously sabotaging her professional
reputation and her personal relationships due to
a latent and repressed fear of failure and
disapproval resulting from some type of deep
seated emotional deficiency instilled upon me in
childhood by my father.

                    MITCH

Grace, for God's sake, I'm only trying to point
out...

                    GRACE

          (cutting him off mid-sentence as
           she walks away)

I am well aware of what you were trying to point
out, which is why I am going to bed. Good
night.

                    MITCH

          (said quietly under his breath)

And she walks away using her anger as a defense
mechanism.

                    GRACE

          (yelling from the background)

I heard that!

                    *Mitch is left alone, sipping
                    his tea somberly.*

                                        CUT TO:

I.2 INT. GRACE'S OFFICE-NEXT MORNING

                    *Grace opens the door to her
                    office and walks in to find,
                    what is obviously a book,
                    gift-wrapped with a red bow
                    sitting on her desk. She
                    unwraps the book to see an
                    ornately bound volume
                    entitled The Framing of the
                    Constitution and The Bill of*

Rights. There is no gift card and she opens the book, quizzically and sits at her desk and starts to read the introduction.

GRACE

I guess someone thinks I need a refresher course!

(laughing to herself)

CUT TO:

I.3 INT. THE COURTROOM - MORNING

Grace enters the courtroom and takes her seat.

BAILIFF

All rise, the Honorable Grace Porter now presiding.

GRACE

Thank you. Good Morning. Please be seated. Court is now in session.

She POUNDS the gavel.

GRACE (CONT'D)

Will the defendants please rise and face the
jury. Mr. Foreman, has your jury agreed upon
your verdicts?

FOREPERSON

We have your Honor.

GRACE

What say you, Mr. Foreman, wherein each of the
six defendants are charged with felonious
destruction of property, are they guilty or not
guilty?

FOREPERSON

Not guilty, your Honor.

GRACE

In that there were five separate counts for each
defendant for the destruction of property, was
your verdict of "not guilty" unanimous across
all counts or do we need to review each count
separately?

FOREPERSON

Unanimous across all five counts, your Honor.

GRACE

So be it recorded. We move on to the next
charges, wherein each of the six defendants are
charged with two misdemeanor counts of engaging
in and conspiracy to engage in a riot, are they
guilty or not guilty?

FOREPERSON

Not guilty, your Honor.

GRACE

In that there were two separate counts for each
defendant, was your "not guilty" verdict
unanimous across both counts or do we need to
review each count separately?

FOREPERSON

Unanimous for both counts, your Honor!

GRACE

Members of the jury hearken to your verdict as
the Court will record it. You, upon your oath,
do say that each of the six defendants are not
guilty of five counts of destruction of
property. So say you, Mr. Foreman. So say you
all members of the jury?

FOREPERSON AND ALL JURORS

(Rise and speak in Unison)

We do, your Honor!

GRACE

And as wherein each of the six defendants are
charged with engaging in and conspiracy to
engage in a riot, you, upon your oath, do say
that the defendants are not guilty. So say you,
Mr. Foreman. So say you all members of the
jury?

FOREPERSON AND ALL JURORS

(Rise and speak in unison)

We do, your Honor!

GRACE

Let the records show that the jury has returned,
in total, 42 not guilty verdicts! Defendants,
Jennifer Armento, Michelle Macchio, Oliver
Harris, Brittne Lawson, Christina Simmons and
Alexei Wood, the jury having returned verdicts
of not guilty on these complaints, the Court
orders that you be discharged and go without day
on these complaints.

Grace POUNDS her gavel!

GRACE (CONT'D)

Members of the jury, during this trial I told
you in my instructions that the verdict was your
responsibility. For that reason, I never
comment on the verdict reached. I appreciate
the seriousness with which you accepted your
responsibilities and reached your decisions.
Your jury duty is now complete. I thank you for
your service! The privilege to be named and

participate in jury service is a critical and founding element of our democracy! Thomas Jefferson said, "I consider trial by jury as the only anchor ever yet imagined by man, by which a government can be held to the principles of its constitution." You will now be escorted back to the jury room where you will be discharged. Court is adjourned!

> *Grace stands and exits.*

> CUT TO:

I.4 EXT. OUTSIDE - SAME TIME

> *There is great excitement outside the courthouse. Michael Pantovere, one of the defendant's attorneys, a tall, serious, outspoken advocate for our Constitution and The Bill of Rights, steps up to the reporter's microphone to speak.*

REPORTER

(You can hear a reporter yell this question from the background)

How does it feel to be exonerated on all charges? Do you feel vindicated that the jury obviously agreed with your right to protest the arrival of this current administration?

PANTOVERE

Justice has been well served here today! My
client was doing nothing more than expressing
her right to free speech and peaceful assembly,
the very essence of the First Amendment. On the
very first day of assuming office, this
administration exercised far reaching authority
in trying not just my client but in also
charging over two hundred other protestors with
crimes that could have resulted in over 60 years
in prison! My client was subjected to
overzealous prosecution by the Justice
Department and the office of the Attorney
General who are trying to set an example for
those who engage in opposition, relying on an
unsuccessful guilt-by-association argument.
Theodore Roosevelt once said, "To announce that
there must be no criticism of the President, or
that we are to stand by the President, right or
wrong, is not only unpatriotic and servile, but
is morally treasonable to the American public."

REPORTER

> (You can hear a reporter again, ask
> this question from the
> background)

This should bring optimism to the remaining
protestors awaiting trial!

PANTOVERE

Yes, it certainly should! When our most basic
freedoms are being questioned and criminalized
than this country has reached a very dark place.
Our democracy is at risk!

> (pauses for effect)

I do not condone violence! The protesters who actually committed acts of violence and destruction have been tried and sentenced or are in the process of being tried accordingly. There is a distinct difference between being a lawbreaker and a protester. Since when has dissent become a crime? It is painfully clear that this has nothing to do with wrongdoing or criminality and everything to do with politics! Why weren't more than a few of the white supremacists protesting in Charlottesville arrested and charged? Every single person in this great country needs to take heed of what is going on and speak up. Please call your Congressmen and complain. Let your voices be heard!

> *Pantovere exits.*

> CUT TO: CLOSE ON

I.5 INT. GRACE'S OFFICE-AFTERNOON

> *Grace is sitting at her desk, and closes her eyes briefly. She takes her "gift book" out of her briefcase, staring at the cover, lost in thought.*

> CUT TO:

> SIDE WINDOW IN THE COURTROOM. DISSOLVE THROUGH THE WINDOW TO THE OTHER SIDE TO INTRODUCE THE

I.6 INT. "THE RED ROOM" WHERE ALL FLASHBACK
SCENES WILL OCCUR - DAY

> *George Washington is reading
> a newspaper. John Adams is
> pacing back and forth.
> Thomas Jefferson, Benjamin
> Franklin, Alexander Hamilton
> and James Madison are all
> seated or standing at various
> locations around the room.*

JOHN ADAMS

(seeming a little befuddled and not
quite sure of his whereabouts)

It would appear that the doctrines of due
process and trial by jury remain intact and
well-functioning in these United States of
America, whatever the date may be...

THOMAS JEFFERSON

Yes, oddly enough indeed!

(chuckling)

Why our lady judge quotes me quite sincerely!
The people of these United States of America can
rely upon and hold high the right of trial by
jury as, a form of democratic involvement in the
administration of criminal justice. Why, I've
heard trial by jury referred to as, the first
privilege of freemen - The noblest article that

ever entered the constitution in a free country
- a jewel whose transcendent luster adds dignity
to human nature.

BENJAMIN FRANKLIN

(said jokingly and as an aside)

And yet, I have also heard it said that, A jury
consists of twelve persons chosen to decide who
has the better lawyer.

(pauses for effect)

As I like to say, A countryman between two
lawyers, is like a fish between two cats!

THOMAS JEFFERSON

As I remember it dear John, evolving from The
Magna Carta and English common law, trial by
jury has dated back as early as the year of 1606
in the state of Virginia.

JOHN ADAMS

The right to trial by jury received formal
recognition in the Massachusetts Body of
Liberties of 1641, shortly followed by
Connecticut, Rhode Island and New York.

THOMAS JEFFERSON

In 1776, Virginia framed the first state
Constitution and specified that in criminal
cases, the defendant had a right to a "speedy
trial by an impartial jury of his vicinage."

With the exception of religious freedoms, no other personal right received as much protection from individual state constitutions. Virginia's was the first permanent state constitution that included among other liberties, freedom of the press.

JOHN ADAMS

(said theatrically and with great
flair)

I just love to remind you that Pennsylvania's Bill of Rights was more comprehensive and ... Massachusetts

(said as an aside)

A state near and dear to my heart, had the most comprehensive state Bill of Rights and was an ideal source of reference in helping to frame the federal version.

BENJAMIN FRANKLIN

(Looking at John Adams half in
disgust and half in amusement)

Simply, mad.... Simply mad!

(pauses for effect)

I am persuaded however; that he (John Adams) means well for his Country, is always an honest Man, often is a wise one, but sometimes and, in some things, absolutely out of his senses.

ALEXANDER HAMILTON

(glaring at Adams)

An inherently erratic character who often lacks control over his impulses.

JOHN ADAMS

There have been many times in my life when I have been so agitated in my own mind as to have no consideration at all of the light in which my words, actions, and even writings would be considered by others... The few traces that remain of me must, I believe, go down to posterity in much confusion and distraction, as my life has been passed.

(pauses for effect)

I must tell you that my wife, bids me tell you that she, "thinks my head, too, a little crack," and I am half of that mind myself.

(pauses for effect)

How is it that I, poor ignorant I, must stand before posterity as differing from all the other great Men of the Age?

(pauses for effect)

I am obnoxious, suspected and unpopular.

JAMES MADISON

Dear gentlemen, let us get back to the topic at hand. As my support for this nauseous project of amendments has grown in magnitude, I have become more convinced that these inalienable rights are critical in ensuring a smooth functioning sovereign state. Initially, I too, had my doubts about amending the Constitution with a set of enumerated rights for fear as what that would purportedly imply about those rights not specifically spelled out. My concern was that, if an enumeration be made of all our rights, will it not be implied that everything omitted is given to the general government?

(said with disgust and aversion)

But did we just hear counsel state that this current administration is, in fact, attempting to repress free speech and the right to peaceful assembly? **Why, that was not what we had in mind!**

(said in perplexity and with great thought)

THOMAS JEFFERSON

Why, I certainly agree James, **that was not what we had in mind at all!** All free and independent men must at all times retain the ability to disagree with their government and gather to do so!

ALEXANDER HAMILTON

Why gentlemen, the Constitution is itself, in every rational sense, and to every useful purpose, a Bill of Rights. Such restraints are implied as we continue our efforts to frame and regulate a government of limited powers and it certainly sounds like this administration is

exercising powers that they do not possess. The
tyrannical manipulations of George III forced us
to stand united and revolt to earn our
independence, creating a democracy and freeing
us from the onerous, cumbersome chains of an
authoritarian dictatorship!

(pauses for effect)

It sounds like this new administration needs a
refresher course in history so that they may be
reminded of the difference between a
dictatorship and a democracy!

(pauses for effect)

My concern all along, has been that a Bill of
Rights would be "dangerous" and "unnecessary"
because it would contain various exceptions to
powers not granted; and, on this very account,
would afford a very colorful pretext to claim
more than were granted, for why declare that
things shall not be done which there is no power
to do?

(pauses for effect)

Why for instance, should it be said that the
LIBERTY of the press shall not be restrained,
when no power is given by which restrictions may
be imposed?

JAMES MADISON

It sounds like that is what we are witnessing
here and it pains me to think that the checks
and balances we worked so hard to create are
being manipulated or ignored all together.

JOHN ADAMS

It is unfathomable that innocent constituents
are being arrested and tried for exercising such
basic freedoms!

ALEXANDER HAMILTON

Government implies the power of making laws. It
is essential to the idea of a law, that it be
attended with a sanction; or, in other words, a
penalty or punishment for disobedience. For if
this is not the case, my friends, why has
government been instituted at all? Because the
passions of men will not conform to the dictates
of REASON and JUSTICE, without constraint.

THOMAS JEFFERSON

We cannot assume that REASON alone will be
enough to steer this country and its citizens
down a path of peace and prosperity.

BENJAMIN FRANKLIN

So convenient a thing it is to be a REASONABLE
creature, since it enables one to find or make a
reason for everything that one has a mind to do!

GEORGE WASHINGTON

        (said factually and with great
            deliberation, as he paces back
            and forth)

I believe that our constituents have become accustomed to the idea that government exists by the consent of the governed,

      (pauses for effect)

that people create government,

      (pauses for effect)

that they do so by written compact,

      (pauses for effect)

that the compact constitutes fundamental law,

      (pauses for effect)

that the government must be subject to such limitations as are necessary for the security of the rights of the people,

      (pauses for effect)

and, usually that the reserved rights of the people are enumerated in a Bill of Rights.

      ALEXANDER HAMILTON

      (Said with great conviction)

The sacred rights of mankind are not to be rummaged for among old parchment or musty records.

      (pauses for effect and for
        emphasis)

They are written... as with a sunbeam,

>   (shifting his glance towards the
>   heaven and extending his arms)

in the whole volume of human nature, by the hand
of divinity itself, and can never be erased or
obscured by mortal power.

                     GEORGE WASHINGTON

While it is entirely unREASONable to assume we
will be in total agreement as to the CONtent and
the INtent of these unprecedented documents of
collective faith, I do think we must all agree
gentlemen, upon the imperative nature of many of
these suggested enumerations, specifically
freedom of speech and of the press,

>   (pauses for effect)

for, if men are to be precluded from offering
their sentiments on a matter which may involve
the most serious and alarming consequences that
can invite the consideration of mankind, REASON
is of no use to us; the freedom of speech may be
taken away, and dumb and silent we may be led
like sheep to the slaughter!

                                          CUT TO:

I.7 INT. RESTAURANT - LATER

>   *Grace and her spirited and*
>   *lively, younger sister,*
>   *Gabrielle, enter the*
>   *restaurant. The host*
>   *recognizes them and kisses*
>   *them both on each cheek.*

                    HOST

Ahh... Senoritas Porter. Welcome tonight, my
lovely ladies!

                         The host leads them to a
                         table and hands each of them
                         a menu.

                    GABRIELLE

Gracias, Amigo! We're both very hungry... And
thirsty!

                    HOST

Of course, I'll send someone right over to take
your order.

                         The waitress comes to the
                         table and takes their order
                         for Margaritas and dinner.
                         Grace checks her phone and
                         reads a text from Mitch sent
                         earlier in the day, inviting
                         her to dinner and realizes
                         that she had never responded.
                         Grace pauses for a moment and
                         leans over and gives her
                         little sister a big sisterly
                         hug and ruffles her hair.

                    GRACE

I'm really proud of you, Gabrielle! Mom and Dad
would be.... are... too! We lead such different
lives and though you know I constantly worry
about your "reckless side," that wild streak

that makes me lose sleep at night, you have this ability to touch and lift up those who need it most!

GABRIELLE

Mom and Dad are likely just proud that I am gainfully employed and not pregnant or on welfare!

GRACE

Don't be so hard on yourself, Gabe! You have a lot to be proud of!

GABRIELLE

You say that today Gracie and yet, tomorrow is another story! You set such high standards for everyone in your life, including yourself, some days I fall far short!

GRACE

Gabe, I'm trying to tell you I couldn't be more proud of you. Can't we leave it at that for just once?

GABRIELLE

Well, I love working with the kids. I can't imagine doing anything else! We're very close to getting spots on several Special Olympics teams for some of our students. I'm so excited for them!

                    GRACE

I was so inspired when I stopped by the school
to see you last week and you were shooting hoops
with one of your students. If you could have
seen the love on that kid's face when he hugged
you...You have such a gift! I could literally
feel your compassion and determination from
across the gym! You must feel such an
incredible sense of accomplishment at the end of
each day and somehow, right now, I feel that
slipping away from me.

                  GABRIELLE

How so?

                    GRACE

Every day seems just like the one before it. I
know I have so much to be thankful for and
believe me, I am! There's just something that
seems to be missing. Of course, I can't have
this conversation with Mitch because we revert
into that doctor-patient psychoanalysis game,
which is painful at every level.

                  GABRIELLE

Maybe you just read too much into everything,
Gracie? Live every moment like it's your last
and maybe you'll come to realize that you're not
missing anything at all!

          (pauses for effect)

Why so maudlin tonight, Gracie? What has
happened to send you on this journey of self-
reflection and self-doubt?

(laughing)

Why all gloom and doom?

GRACE

I think it's more of an "identity crisis."

GABRIELLE

Stemming from what? What happened?

GRACE

Well, Mitch and I had an argument the other
night and he in so many words, no, he just came
right out and said that my conservative legal
inclinations were stemming from some type of
latent need for Dad's approval.

GABRIELLE

Wow, remind me not to call on either one of you
guys if I'm looking for light, cheerful
conversation.

(laughing)

Geez.... So what exactly is it that sets Mitch
off on his need for psychoanalysis?

(gesturing with her hands)

Knowing you two brain trusts as well as I do...

(pauses for effect)

So, you're sitting there having a pleasant, normal, everyday conversation about, oh, I don't know, the moral degradation of American youths or food and water shortages in evolving third world countries or...

GRACE

(laughing and cutting her off mid sentence)

Very funny. We were actually just having a conversation regarding the anticipated first round of verdicts for the inauguration day protesters. He believes my conservative political viewpoints all center around not wanting to disappoint Dad's legacy.

GABRIELLE

Well, sis, you are your Father's daughter in many more ways than just that. Doesn't seem so unusual to me? So, the question is, why does it bother YOU so much?

GRACE

(sighs and shrugs her shoulders)

I guess I'm personally having a really hard time finding ways to agree with this administration. The Republican party controls the Senate right now and I'm really starting to see that it is a real..., nothing is getting done. The mandate of Congress is to protect our Constitution and defend our country. I'm having some real concerns.

                    GABRIELLE

Whoa... This is big - like a total change in your political ideology? Is it Mitch just rubbing off on you with all of his liberal views or did you come to this conclusion all by yourself?

                     GRACE

No, it's all my own doing. Why does it have to be left or right? I hate that everything has become so polarized and politicized. I've always appreciated that the end results of spirited debate should be thoughtful deliberation that leads to consensus, you know, agreement!

                    GABRIELLE

It's not just you, Gracie! I recently read an article that something like over 65% of Americans are exhausted with polarized politics. It's the new norm!

          (pauses for effect)

It's not like you need to come to this decision overnight. So much could happen over the next couple of years. I still remain confident that we will have a woman President one day but most importantly, I just want our country to be peaceful and prosperous!

GRACE

Dad always voted along party lines, no matter
what and so I guess I followed suit because I
wasn't sure. So in regards to following in
Dad's footsteps, in this instance, Mitch is
right!

(pauses for effect)

Back in the day, no matter what side of the
aisle you sat on, great strides were made that
continued to move our country onward and upward.
Now it's just gridlock. Vitriolic discourse.
We, as a country, are better than this!

GABRIELLE

(laughing)

Ugh...

GRACE

What's wrong?

GABRIELLE

Leave it to my Mensa member sister

GRACE

What?

GABRIELLE

(mimicking her sister in a high-
pitched voice)

"It's all vitriolic discourse."

(laughing)

Why can't you just call it out for what it is?
Mudslinging, backstabbing, character
assassination, name calling, slimy, greasy
politics!

(pauses for effect)

So, getting back to our previous topic of
conversation, does Mitch know about your
potential defection?

GRACE

No, I haven't discussed it with him yet.

GABRIELLE

Why not? It could actually be a monumental
shift in bringing you closer together!

GRACE

Oh crap!

GABRIELLE

What's wrong?

GRACE

He texted earlier today when I was in court
asking me to dinner tonight and I meant to get
back to him on my way here to meet you and.... I
forgot, damn it!

GABRIELLE

Be honest with yourself. You two have been at a
stalemate now for what? A year, maybe more.
Mitch is the most incredible thing that has ever
happened to you and I think you're afraid of
failure again.

GRACE

It's not that I'm afraid of failure, but I
believe in long-term relationships that may not
last forever. Give me a break, Gabe. I already
have one shrink in my life, I really don't need
one more!

        (laughing)

GABRIELLE

Kyle was a mistake that never should have
happened. At the very least, you know what you
don't want to end up with again... Move on.
Mitch is an incredibly patient and understanding
guy and he is waiting for you to reach out to
him, really be there for him, but even he.... Is
not a saint.

GRACE

You paint a bleak picture.

(sighing)

I love him. He is all that you say he is,
though you left out stubborn and hard-headed.

GABRIELLE

You see, that's just what I mean!

(talking with her hands
expressively)

A match made in heaven!

(laughing)

Sometimes, I think that's part of it. You're
two peas in a pod in so many ways. If not you,
eventually there will be somebody else for him.
He's yours to lose.

GABRIELLE (CONT'D)

Look, why don't you go surprise ole Mitch and
just stop over unexpectedly? I'm sure he'd be
happy to see you and happy to know you were
thinking about him and wanting to move past your
little lover's quarrel!

GRACE

Well, I don't know, I have to be in early
tomorrow.

GABRIELLE

Come on, drop me off at my car and be gone with you!

They stand and exit.

CUT TO:

I.8 INT. - THE RED ROOM - EVENING

> *Alexander Hamilton and Benjamin Franklin are standing in a corner of the room.*

BENJAMIN FRANKLIN

Cupid's arrow is certainly having a difficult time casting its magic spell as we witness this course of events. The fellow seems smitten enough, but our lady judge seems a bit, well... distracted.

(pauses for effect)

Our lady judge needs to realize that, human felicity is produced not so much by great pieces of good fortune that seldom happen, as by little advantages that occur every day. The younger sister seems to have a better understanding of this concept and displays a certain vivacity, quite appealing and enchanting!

ALEXANDER HAMILTON

Why, she's young enough to be your granddaughter
or once again removed from that, Benjamin, you
devil you!

(slapping him on the shoulder)

BENJAMIN FRANKLIN

Why Alexander...

(said chuckling and with good
nature)

I'm simply trying to point out the virtues I
perceive to be present in this young woman's
person, as when the brightest of female virtues
shine among other perfections of body and mind
in the same person, it makes the woman more
lovely than an angel.

(pauses for effect)

Though my years surely do find me at an advanced
age, I can only ask to be allowed to carry on
with grace and in control of my virtues! To
quote one of my favorite old songs: "May I
govern my passions with an absolute sway, Grow
wiser and better as my strength wears away,
Without gout, or stone, by a gentle decay."

CUT TO:

I.9 INT. - HELEN'S OFFICE - DAY

*Grace walks into Helen
Hutching's office and she and
Helen, a regal-looking woman*

with silver-gray hair,
embrace warmly.

HELEN

Hello, my lovely, you stay away too long! You
look more like your Mother every time I see you.
How's your little hellion of a sister?

GRACE

Gabrielle? She is wonderful and brilliant in
her own special way!

HELEN

(said laughing and in a joking way)

Are we talking about the same person?

GRACE

Yes, she's been exercising extreme self-control
lately!

HELEN

Not our Gabe? Sit and eat. I'm sure your
schedule rarely allows for a leisurely lunch and
the company of an old friend. We haven't had a
chance to talk in such a long while my angel and
yet, I know you like my own. What troubles you
so, my dear?

GRACE

I feel like I'm having a professional, mid-life
crisis. You know how I struggled in the DA's
office until I got elected to my current seat?
Always struggling, right versus wrong, good,
bad, black, white. Oh God, I even drive myself
crazy! I've got opening arguments tomorrow
against one of the organizers of the
Charlottesville, "Unite the Right" rally, which
is going to be all over the front pages. I've
never presided over a case with such
unprecedented and inflammatory subject matter
and the media is going to have a field day with
this one! No matter which way the jury rules,
and no matter how tough or lenient my sentence
is, an appeal is likely!

HELEN

The apples don't fall far from the tree, my
dear.

GRACE

You know, Mitch accused me of trying to appease
Daddy's legacy too! Well, I don't think that's
what I'm doing!

HELEN

I think I can safely speak for both Mitch and
myself, when I say, when you have such a
powerful man involved in your upbringing, how
can you not be swayed to lean in the direction
of what you're most familiar and accustomed to?

GRACE

Well, maybe, to a certain extent, but on the one
hand, I have the constraints of the legal system
that are binding. The Constitution and the Bill
of Rights were meant to regulate and steer the
actions of this country indefinitely. Just
because I don't share a belief or an expression
of opinion, doesn't mean that a person doesn't
have the right to openly express that opinion!

HELEN

Are you saying that you will somehow be able to
professionally rationalize the actions of this
monster? The actions of a white supremacist,
whose deliberate and well thought out plans for
violence and destruction ultimately led to a
mother and her two children being murdered?

GRACE

This has nothing to do with my personal
opinions, Helen. But precedence will play a key
role and I, along with the jury, will be bound
by its oversight.

HELEN

Precedence withstanding Grace, you must also be
able to look yourself in the mirror at the end
of the day! The person is more important than
the precedence!

GRACE

No one feels that pressure more than I do,
Helen! I know all too well that I have my own
self-respect and professional credibility to
keep in mind.

HELEN

Hmmm... ultimately, I think respect is the
driver. If you lose your self-respect, you have
nothing. Arm yourself with knowledge and faith,
my dear, and you will prevail.

GRACE

(with tears in her eyes)

If I close my eyes, I could see Mom saying those
exact same words to me. How I miss her!

HELEN

A better friend, I never had. I miss her too!
We're so proud of you!

GRACE

Are you? I'm not so sure you should be. I'm
not so sure about anything right now.

HELEN

I think you're absolutely sure of what you need
to do and that just scares you. Never be too
proud to admit your fears.

(pauses for effect)

Call me next week and let's plan for that
dashing man of yours to accompany you to dinner
at the beach house. Stu's been asking about you
lately.

GRACE

We'd love to Helen. Thanks so much! You always
make me feel so much better!

HELEN

You can bring that crazy sister of yours if
she's free. Just tell her the pool boys off
limits this time!

(laughter)

GRACE

We'll look forward to dinner. I'll be in touch.

Grace and Helen embrace.
Grace exits.

CUT TO:

I.10 INT. THE RED ROOM - CLOSE UP - BENJAMIN
FRANKLIN

*The stage is dark with a
spotlight on Franklin.*

BENJAMIN FRANKLIN

Our lady judge certainly seems to be having an
internal struggle with her virtues and if given
the luxury, I would offer to her that, in
reality, there is perhaps no one of our natural
passions so hard to subdue as pride; disguise
it, struggle with it, beat it down, stifle it,
mortify it as much as one pleases, it is still
alive and will every now and then peep out and
show itself.

(pauses for effect)

How few there are who have courage enough to own
their faults, or resolution enough to mend them.

(pauses for effect)

One's true happiness depends more upon one's
judgement of one's self, or a consciousness of
rectitude in action and intention, than the
approbation of those few, who judge impartially,
than the applause of the unthinking,
undiscerning multitude.

CUT TO:

ACT II

IRONY

II.1 INT. THE COURTROOM - MORNING

> *The bailiff enters. Before the courtroom doors are closed, shouting and protesting can be heard outside the doors.*

BAILIFF

All rise, the Honorable Grace Porter presiding.

> *Grace enters the courtroom, takes her seat and POUNDS the gavel.*

GRACE

Please be seated. Court is now in session. Today we are gathered to hear the opening arguments in The Commonwealth of Virginia versus Noah Lester, d/b/a

> (she pauses and makes a half questionable/half disgusted expression)

Noah's Alt-Right Knights, a/k/a Noah's ARK.

> (there is considerable noise in the courtroom - *Grace POUNDS the gavel*)

Are you prepared to give opening statements, counsel?

                    SNAYDER/PANTOVERE

> (both rise in unison and reply simultaneously)

We are your Honor.

                    GRACE

Counsel, approach the bench, please.

> *The attorney for the prosecution, Michael Pantovere, and the crafty-looking attorney for the defense, Leonard Snayder, approach the bench.*

                    GRACE (CONT'D)

Mr. Snayder, I've never had the privilege...

> (said with some degree of ridicule)

Of your presence in my courtroom before, have I?

                    SNAYDER

No, your Honor.

GRACE

Far be it from me to comment on your choice of
cases. But I warn you, Mr. Snayder, your
reputation precedes you and I will not have you
turn my courtroom into a mockery. Using First
Amendment protection for a criminal charge of
aiding and abetting in an act of domestic
terrorism that ultimately led to the murder of a
mother and her two young children, coupled with
a conspiracy charge, is a far stretch; however,
your country gives you the right to due process.

(pauses for effect)

That being said, I trust you will prepare
accordingly and to the letter of the law. Media
attention is going to be fierce and if you try
to use that to your advantage in any way, it
will be a big mistake. Let's not make this a
battle of the constitutionality of the
constitution, Mr. Snayder. The documents are
intact and function optimally as a barometer for
regulating **JUSTICE**, the actions of our citizens.
Right versus wrong!

SNAYDER

Yes, your Honor. I will heed your advice in
these proceedings.

(also said with some degree of
ridicule)

GRACE

Step away, counselors. Let's get started, shall
we?

The attorneys return to their seats and Snayder PATS his client on the back.

SNAYDER

(said in a hushed tone, under his breath, to his seated client, Noah Lester)

Don't worry my friend. She's all talk! She's about as tough as my manicurist!

(laughing)

Right versus wrong? What planet does she live on? **JUSTICE** is truly only another word for the act of convincing, the art of manipulation, the end result of winning versus losing! Why these "great" documents are merely the products of a bunch of old, long-winded, white-wigged ideologues, looking for a place in the history books!

NOAH LESTER

I don't know, she sounds pretty convincing to me!

SNAYDER

Piece of cake, Noah, my boy. You could have done a lot worse as far as the judge assigned to your case. She's perfect...not married, no kids, cold broad. We're in good shape here!

PATTING Noah Lester on the back.

GRACE

Very well, Mr. Pantovere, let's get started.

PANTOVERE

The Western District Court of the Commonwealth of Virginia, charges the defendant, Noah Lester, d/b/a Noah's ARK with conspiracy to commit a felony and in aiding and abetting in the murders of Susan Leiberman Walker 42, Hope Walker 12 and Bryant Walker 8, who were killed, when coconspirator, Alan Shields, also a member of the Alt-Right Knights, drove his vehicle into a group of civilians and counter-protestors, as a direct result of the instructions and urging of Mr. Lester and his social media correspondence prior to the incident.

(pauses for effect)

Mr. Shields was recently found guilty of First Degree Murder and other charges and sentenced to life in prison plus 419 years and also recently plead guilty to numerous hate crimes and is awaiting sentencing for those charges. Mr. Lester, Mr. Shields and several other of their white supremacist cohorts and consortiums are also facing numerous civil and criminal charges in several other separate cases, as a result of their premeditated, violent and destructive behavior at the Charlottesville rally.

(pauses for effect)

The evidence provided will prove that, the four necessary elements required to prove guilt beyond a reasonable doubt, are present, specifically: A crime was committed; that the

accused aided, counseled, commanded, induced or
procured the person committing the crime; that
the accused acted with the intent to facilitate
the crime; and that the accused acted before the
crime was committed.

(pauses for effect)

Conspiracy charges require an extra element of
evidence that proves an individual or
individuals were in agreement to commit a crime
rather than just to aid or abet a crime. We are
asking that the defendant be charged with the
maximum criminal penalties available, and other
relief that the Court deems necessary and just.
The state intends to prove Mr. Lester's guilt
beyond a reasonable doubt.

GRACE

Thank you, Mr. Pantovere. Mr. Snayder, proceed,
please.

SNAYDER

(Rises and replies somewhat
mockingly)

Thank you, your Honor. Ladies and gentlemen of
the jury, my client, Noah Lester, sits here
before you today, an innocent man who was doing
nothing more than exercising his rights
guaranteed under the First Amendment. Alan
Shields, the actual driver of the vehicle that
killed the Walker family members, has been
charged and convicted of first degree murder and
other charges and has been sentenced accordingly
for those charges and is awaiting sentencing for

the other hate crime charges. He alone, is
responsible for his actions, not my client!
People can say provocative things in the heat of
the moment! It is up to those who are
listening, the recipients, to choose how to
respond.

(pauses for effect)

As you ladies and gentlemen of the jury are
aware, the law states, innocent until proven
guilty. Mark Twain once said, "In our country,
we have those three unspeakably precious things:
freedom of speech, freedom of conscience and the
providence to never practice either."

(laughter in the courtroom)

However, my client, Noah Lester, did in fact,
exercise these unspeakably precious rights.
There is no law against assembling to protest
and stand up for your beliefs and the rally he
attended was given the proper permit in advance
by the city of Charlottesville. I thought it
might be helpful to refresh everyone's memories
who are here today, not as attorneys, but as
jurors or interested bystanders. The First
Amendment states that, "Congress shall make no
law respecting an establishment of religion, or
prohibiting the free exercise thereof or
abridging the freedom of speech, or of the
press; or of the right of the people peaceably
to assemble, and to petition the government for
a redress of grievances."

(pauses for effect)

So while you may not agree with any of his
beliefs or ideologies, the First Amendment of
the Bill of Rights was intended to protect

minority interests from persecution. It is a
bill of restraints on the United States
government to guard against abuses of power. I
intend to prove that my client, Noah Lester, is
innocent of all charges being brought against
him by the Commonwealth of Virginia. I thank
you members of the jury for performing one of
the most important functions entrusted upon you
by the Constitution of this great and free
nation.

> (motioning with his hand in a
> sweeping gesture)

Your Honor...

> *Snayder takes his seat.*

GRACE

Thank you, Mr. Snayder.

PANTOVERE

I concur, that The Bill of Rights was written to
protect expression by the minority, but
according to one of our great framers, James
Madison, "it stands to reason that, there are
several classes of speech or of publication,
some of which were not intended to be
categorized under the umbrella of First
Amendment protection." So these great documents
have consistently been used and used
successfully over the course of these centuries
as a framework, which is heavily relied upon,
but given interpretive latitude.

> (pauses for effect)

Court rulings have repeatedly recognized, that the First Amendment's right to petition the government is cut from the same cloth as other guarantees of that Amendment, and is an assurance of a particular freedom of expression, but... It does not relieve citizens from liability arising out of it. The First Amendment does not provide absolute immunity, but qualified immunity, where the charges can be disputed and proven false beyond a shadow of a doubt. The U.S. Constitution establishes a floor under our rights, a bottom level, not a ceiling.

(pauses for effect)

It was also once said, that the person who has freedom of the press, owns one. Contemporary social media platforms allow for those who have their own web sites, blogs, etc., to quickly establish far reaching audiences and serve as a mechanism to rapidly disseminate information that can have profound influences on their viewers. Clandestine chat platforms such as "Discord" also provided a channel for private, "secret" communications between Mr. Lester and other white supremacists in their planning of the "Unite the Right" rally in Charlottesville. We, as a country, can no longer allow the technologically savvy, Alt-Right fringe groups unfettered access to tools that allow them to get away with MURDER, literally!

                    SNAYDER

Objection! Your Honor, counsel is convicting my client even before we have finished opening arguments!

GRACE

Sustained! Watch your wording, Mr. Pantovere!

PANTOVERE

John Adams once said, "A nation of laws grew out of a nation of men," and out of respect for their enduring footprint, I, as an officer of the court and of the judicial system of the United States of America, am compelled to uphold their Honor and their written word.

(pauses for effect)

The issue at hand is the imminent danger posed by white supremacist groups, specifically, Mr. Lester's, his social media platforms and the very explicit instructions disseminated prior to, and during the Charlottesville rally and in its' aftermath!

CUT TO: CLOSE ON

II.2 INT. THE RED ROOM - SAME TIME

The stage is dark with a spotlight on Adams.

JOHN ADAMS

Hmmm... A nation of laws grew out of a nation of men, I did say that, didn't I?

(said excitedly and pacing back and forth, jabbing at the air)

Brilliant, brilliant in its own right for succinctly summarizing our contributions to the founding of this great nation and the laws that guide it!

>   (pauses for effect and said with
>   great contempt)

But, did I just hear that modern-day Judas refer to us as a bunch of old, long-winded, white-wigged ideologues? Why, if I were a lesser sort, I believe I would be rather insulted right now!

>   CUT TO:

II.3 INT. - BACK TO COURTROOM - SAME TIME

>   PANTOVERE

A significant extent of the charges in this case stem from the planning, execution and incitement to violence at the Charlottesville rally, that led to the riot and ultimate actions of Alan Shields, who willfully drove his vehicle into the Walker family and a group of civilians and counter-protestors. Therefore, it is imperative that we view the tape of the actual incident as it was occurring, as well as have a brief overview of the events both before and after the incident and then follow up with the specific social media conversations that were occurring up to and after the incident, when the tragedies occurred.

>   GRACE

Understandable counselor, please proceed.

PANTOVERE

Ladies and gentlemen of the jury, the contents
of this videotape are graphic and disturbing and
will likely be offensive and parts of it may
be...

SNAYDER

(cutting him off mid sentence)

Objection! Your Honor, counsel is attempting to
color the jury's opinion prior to their even
having an opportunity to view the evidence!

GRACE

Sustained! Mr. Pantovere, I understand your
concern for the more faint of heart here, but
the jurors are aware of the nature of this case
and are likely to have anticipated the necessity
of such a viewing.

PANTOVERE

Of course, thank you, your Honor. I'll proceed
with greater caution.

GRACE

Continue, please.

PANTOVERE

Ladies and gentlemen of the jury, I was simply
trying to stress the need for you to pay careful

and constant attention to this videotape in its entirety, for the rest of this case relies heavily upon your doing so. I submit this to the court, as labeled "Exhibit A." Bailiff, please roll the tape.

Play a brief recording of a newscast that highlights the car assault/vehicular manslaughter and mayhem during the Charlottesville tragedy over speakers

PANTOVERE (CONT'D)

Ladies and gentlemen of the jury, as you have just witnessed, the Walker family met a terrible fate in this very deliberate act of domestic terrorism, with the only survivor being the husband, Tyrone Walker. He lost his entire family due to this act of senseless violence, hatred and bigotry.

(pauses for effect)

Let me just reiterate some of the messages distributed amongst Mr. Lester's social media platforms prior to the attack, regarding the Walker family: Specifically, in a smaller May 2017 rally held in Charlottesville, Mr. Lester singled the Walker family out of the crowd, evidently, because they were a multi-racial family and Mr. Walker was wearing a yarmulke. Mr. Lester got right in their faces, spat on them and referred to them as "a kiked-up-nigger experiment." He then posted this same caption under a photo of them which was posted on his social media platforms. Mr. Lester then proceeded to post other photos of the Walker

family, as well as other very personal family
details, including their address, occupations,
employers, children's schools and their house of
worship. Mr. Lester along with his fellow
fringe groups spent months organizing and
instructing their membership to come to
Charlottesville and to make sure that they were
armed. The Walker family was marked prey ladies
and gentlemen of the jury, they didn't stand a
chance.

SNAYDER

(standing up to interrupt his
adversary)

Your Honor, ladies and gentlemen of the jury.
These proceedings are a gross abuse of our legal
system and an egregious waste of taxpayer's
money and time. In the widely publicized
"Nuremberg File" trials, antiabortionists won
the right to run a website which publicized
abortion provider's personal information,
resulting in the death of seven abortionists.

PANTOVERE

(standing up and shouting in
exasperation)

Objection, your Honor! Move to strike that
reference from the court transcripts! That
verdict was subsequently overturned by the Ninth
Circuit federal appeals court in California. It
was determined that the "Wanted Posters"
published online detailing the personal contact
information of abortion doctors, followed by

killings was sufficient to strip the defendants
of First Amendment protection.

                    GRACE

So stricken! Mr. Snayder, I am familiar with
that ruling, as well! I hope you have a very
quick explanation for your creative
interpretation of these court rulings. I have
held counsel in contempt for much less egregious
misrepresentations.

                    SNAYDER

Your Honor, counsel failed to mention that as a
general rule, First Amendment protection
assertions need to be independently reviewed to
determine its merit or lack thereof. The
"fighting words" doctrine of the First Amendment
gives protection to my client.

                    GRACE

Overruled! A far stretch of an explanation and
you are trying my patience. Mr. Pantovere, do
you have anything further to add?

                    PANTOVERE

Yes, your Honor. First of all, the "fighting
words" doctrine cannot be used as a protection
here because the language used was certainly
insulting epithets, uttered face to face and
likely to provoke retaliation.

GRACE

Sustained! Sit down and zip it, Mr. Snayder!

PANTOVERE

Another pertinent detail is that the permit that
the white supremacist groups received was
ACTUALLY only for August 12th at Emancipation
Park in Charlottesville. The torchlit parade on
the evening of August 11, prior to the next
day's murderous incident, and I quote, "was a
secret arrangement," with said fringe groups and
protesters gathering behind The University of
Virginia's gymnasium in preparation for their
march on the Rotunda. Mr. Lester is an alumnus
of this great and historic University. I guess
somehow he believed this would be some type of a
well-received symbolic gesture to his Alma
Mater?

(pauses for effect)

They lit their torches in direct violation of
UVA's open fire laws. One coconspirator shared
on their top-secret Discord platform that "Tiki
torches are the last stand for implicit
whiteness." And also said that, "our country is
being usurped by a foreign tribe, called the
Jews." They then began their torchlit march to
the Rotunda and down to the Jefferson Statue.

(pauses for effect)

Yes, you heard me right, THOMAS JEFFERSON's
Statue! Chanting racial slurs that included:
"Jews will not replace us" and "White lives
matter!" They barked like dogs and performed
Nazi salutes. They encountered counter-

protesters at the Jefferson statue and surrounded them, denying any route for escape. This was where the violence began. They used their torches as weapons, with one white supremacist shouting, "The heat here is nothing compared to what you're going to get in the ovens."

> (pauses for effect and is visibly
> shaken)

I don't think I need to go any further here, do I ladies and gentlemen of the jury?

> (pauses for effect)

Yes, that's right! Thomas Jefferson's Statute! The Father of The Declaration of Independence, who also just happens to be the founder of The University of Virginia. They fought for our freedom and then they had to fight for our unity!

> (pauses for effect)

Mr. Lester, you betray all of the good that he fought for. I look forward to presenting the very disturbing facts of this case to the jury gathered here today and thank you in advance for your service. I have nothing further, your Honor.

> CUT TO: CLOSE ON

II.4 INT. THE RED ROOM - SAME TIME

> *The stage is dark with a*
> *spotlight on Thomas*
> *Jefferson, who is alone,*
> *sitting at a desk with his*

*head in his hands, rubbing
his eyes as if to be
wondering if he really could
have heard or seen these
courtroom proceedings to be
real.*

THOMAS JEFFERSON

(stands ceremoniously and speaks
with great deliberateness holding
a scroll of the Declaration of
Independence in his hands, he
starts to read)

"...We hold these truths to be self-evident,
that ALL MEN ARE CREATED EQUAL. That they are
endowed by their Creator with certain
UNALIENABLE Rights, that among these are **LIFE**,
LIBERTY and the pursuit of **HAPPINESS**..."

*George Washington and John
Adams walk in and each place
a hand on one of Jefferson's
shoulders.*

THOMAS JEFFERSON (CONT'D)

Why with God as my witness, I cannot comprehend
that the passage of time would reveal such
heathen tendencies amongst our citizenry. **THIS
WAS NOT WHAT WE HAD IN MIND!**

(slamming his fists on the desk in
an uncharacteristic show of
anger)

We fought for our freedom from England to stand up AGAINST repression and for hopes of a new world in the best possible manner that we could achieve in our day!

(pauses for effect)

GEORGE WASHINGTON

Why Thomas, I also penned a very sincere and heartfelt welcome of worship and citizenry to the Hebrew congregation in Newport, Rhode Island, stating that he, who dwell in this land, continue to merit and enjoy the good will of the other inhabitants; while everyone shall sit in safety under his own vine and fig tree, and there shall be none to make him afraid.

THOMAS JEFFERSON

And no less these nauseous events originated at my beloved University of Virginia! Oh, how I toiled for her inception! How I toiled for her construction and creation! It was supposed to be an academical village based on discussion, collaboration and enlightenment, not hatred and intolerance!

(pauses for effect)

One of my proudest accomplishments, that provided a foundation for me to combine my love of architecture with my love of education! It has always been my belief that education engrafts a new man on the native stock, and improves what in his nature is vicious and perverse into qualities of virtue and social worth. So how could education have done the

exact opposite for this Lester fellow, resulting
in a mind full of ignorance and intolerance?

> (pauses for effect, collecting
> himself and his emotions)

A Bill of Rights is meant to serve as a citadel
of freedoms to protect every constituent, be he
poor or of great wealth. But there must be
judicious efforts made by those in the judiciary
to check its abuse and abasement. Our lady
judge and the commonwealth's attorney seem to
have adequate control over these proceedings and
we can only pray that the very essence of these
critical protections will not be inappropriately
twisted to somehow provide a legal defense for
evil, for promoting violence and murder!

GEORGE WASHINGTON

Love of power and proneness to abuse it...
predominate in the human heart.

> *Benjamin Franklin enters the
> room.*

BENJAMIN FRANKLIN

And yet our Constitution, the embodiment of
democracy and emancipation from the shackles of
tyranny from King George and England prohibits
Congress from passing any law that abolished or
restricted the **odious bargain with sin** we know
as slavery, indentured servitude, until 1808.
Article 1, Section 9.

> (pauses for effect)

As the years have passed, my own personal
opinions towards our Negro citizens and their
God-given right to emancipation has been
completely transformed, hence my signature on
the recently submitted petition from my Quaker
group, to the floors of Congress for debate and
deliberation. Subsequently, I have freed all of
my own slaves. Why Thomas, your esteemed
Declaration clearly stated that it was not
possible that one man should have property on
person of another.

THOMAS JEFFERSON

Yes, Benjamin, your words ring true, but our
young union is too tender and confronted with
uncertainties. If we are to endure, we must
give equal consideration to our Southern states
whose prosperity is entwined with the ongoing
access to the slave trade.

(pauses for effect)

Our Constitution provides for an eventual end to
the practice, but for the time being, we need to
give credence to our Southern brothers. It is
the only chance we have to move forward.

(pauses for effect)

Why the census confirms that the slave trade
continues to decrease in our Northern states and
I have every confidence that this trend will
continue.

*Alexander Hamilton enters the
room.*

ALEXANDER HAMILTON

Why Jefferson, how suspect that the ideals you
espoused in your "esteemed Declaration" are
diametrically opposed to those that you practice
in your own agrarian labors at Monticello.
Hypocrisy is not lost on you or your tenet of
agrarian efficiency with the help of a stable of
slaves of your own. You talk one way, you live
another. The words of an Angel, the deeds of a
Devil.

THOMAS JEFFERSON

And yet Hamilton, you have conducted
transactions for the purchase and transfer of
slaves on behalf of your in-laws, so your hands
are not as clean as you profess. We have done
what we have needed to do to move this union
forward. You mischaracterize my situation and
long-term intentions. We will phase out slavery
as our country gains momentum, achieves
solidarity and expands our territory.

GEORGE WASHINGTON

Democracy is a fragile thing. We are faced with
a no win situation. If we include a provision
to end slavery in our Constitution, the years of
hardships we faced in our revolution, our fight
for freedom from England will be lost. Our
Southern states threaten secession over this
complex and combustible issue.

BENJAMIN FRANKLIN

But George, you must concur that slavery is incongruous with our revolutionary principles.

GEORGE WASHINGTON

Our union will be nullified and our victories in the revolution will all have been for naught if we allow for this debate to continue in the present. Collectively, we are doing our best to be as forward thinking as possible. I clearly foresee that nothing but the rooting out of slavery can perpetuate the existence of our union. We can only hope and pray, that our future generation moves this nation forward in peace and prosperity, with **LIBERTY** and **JUSTICE** for all!

BENJAMIN FRANKLIN

A good conscience is a continual Christmas!

> *The stage goes dark with a spotlight shining on Jefferson.*

THOMAS JEFFERSON

I tremble for my Country when I reflect that God is just; that his justice cannot sleep forever.

> (echo this sentence several times as the stage remains dark)

> *James Madison enters the stage. The lights come back on.*

JAMES MADISON

Dear Benjamin, I agree with your assessment.
Slavery is dishonorable to the American
character. Slavery is a Moral, and political
Evil, and that Whoever brings forward in the
Respective States, some General, rational and
Liberal plan, for the Gradual Emancipation of
Slaves, will deserve Well of his Country - yet I
think it is very improper, at this time, to
introduce it in Congress. We need consensus
between the North and the South to realize
unification. Each state has the right to
address and delegitimize slavery in their state
constitutions, as Vermont, Pennsylvania,
Massachusetts, New Hampshire, Connecticut and
Rhode Island have done, rendering slavery
illegal. We must temporarily focus on other
issues if we are to present a unified front.
Issues surrounding slavery are at the core of
our divisiveness, with the potential to destroy
our union. One day, all of our Negro brothers
will be emancipated. We currently could not
withstand a war with our Southern brothers, we
are still regaining our strength from the
aftermath of our revolution.

BENJAMIN FRANKLIN

Mankind are very odd creatures: One half
censure what they practice, the other half
practice what they censure; the rest always say
and do as they ought.

THOMAS JEFFERSON

Good gentlemen, please let us return to the
topic of the Bill of Rights. As we amble

towards consensus, I am now convinced more than ever, that a Bill of Rights, though controversy is sure to arise, as is evident by the trial proceedings we witness here today, is what the people are entitled to against every government on earth, general or particular, and what no just government should refuse or rest on inference.

ALEXANDER HAMILTON

(said with exasperation and sarcasm)

Ugh, Thomas if you are not the last of the Utopian visionaries, I don't know who is.

(rolling his eyes)

It is the plan of the men of this stamp to frighten the people with ideal bugbears, in order to mould them to their own purposes. The increasing cry of these designing croakers is, my friends, your liberty is invaded.

(speaking with his hands and gesturing theatrically)

BENJAMIN FRANKLIN

There are croakers in every country, always boding its ruin.

THOMAS JEFFERSON

I am certainly not an advocate for frequent and untried changes in laws and constitutions. Why,

these documents were penned to allow for such
minor...

(pauses for effect)

Adjustments... and calibrations along the way...
I think moderate imperfections had better be
borne with; because, when once known, we
accommodate ourselves to them, and find
practical means of correcting their ill effects.
But I know also that laws and institutions must
go hand in hand with the progress of the human
mind...

(spoken with great conviction)

We might as well require a man to wear still the
coat which fitted him as a boy, as civilized
society to remain ever under the regimen of
their barbarous ancestors.

(he pauses in reflection)

Some men look at Constitutions with
sanctimonious reverence, and deem them like the
ark of the covenant, too sacred to be touched.
They ascribe to the men of the preceding age a
wisdom more than human, and suppose what they did
to be beyond amendment... no society can make a
perpetual constitution...The earth belongs to
the living and not the dead. Law is only a
means. Government is only a means. Life,
liberty and the pursuit of happiness - these are
the ends.

ALEXANDER HAMILTON

I fear for the potential inability of this
document to cover the infinite realm of rights

required to be comprehensive and instead, ponder
the ramifications of what is sure to be a finite
enumeration, at best. An imperfect Bill of
Rights is worse than none at all.

THOMAS JEFFERSON

A Bill of Rights will be effective and if it
inconveniently cramps the government, the effect
will be short-lived and remediable, while the
inconveniences of not having a Bill of Rights
could be permanent, afflicting and irreparable.

(pauses for effect)

If there were no such document, this Lester
fellow would have nothing to answer to but his
own moral compass, imperiling our citizenry and
terrorizing his fellow man!

JOHN ADAMS

Whoever would found a state and make proper laws
for the government of it must presume that all
men are bad by nature.

JAMES MADISON

It may be a reflection on human nature that such
devices should be necessary to control the
abuses of government. But what is government
itself but the greatest of all reflections on
human nature?

(pauses for effect and looks up
towards the heavens)

If men were angels, no government would be necessary.

(pauses for effect)

If angels were to govern men, neither external nor internal controls on government would be necessary.

(pauses for effect)

In framing a government which is to be administered by men over men, the great difficulty lies in this: you must first enable the government to control the governed, and in the next place oblige it to control itself.

ALEXANDER HAMILTON

There is no CERTAINTY that this country would operate at a deficit if no such enumerations were enacted!

BENJAMIN FRANKLIN

In this world, nothing can be said to be CERTAIN...

(pauses for effect)

Except for... Death and taxes.

(chuckling to himself)

> John Adams walks over to
> Thomas Jefferson and once
> again puts his hand on one of
> Jefferson's shoulders. The
> lights dim and the stage

darkens, shining a spotlight on Jefferson and Adams.

JOHN ADAMS

When people talk of the freedom of writing, speaking or thinking I cannot choose but laugh. No such thing ever existed. No such thing now exists; but I hope it will exist. But it must be hundreds of years after you and I shall write and speak no more.

CUT TO:

II.5 INT. RESTAURANT - EVENING

The two sisters enter the restaurant.

BARTENDERS

Well, well, well. Top of the evening to you ladies! It's a pleasure to see you both again!

GRACE

Too much work, not enough fun. We figured you could help us out with the fun part. Two extra dirty Martinis and the sooner the better!

The two sisters sit at the bar and the bartender brings them their drinks.

GABRIELLE

OK...sister...scoop me,

(pauses)

As able...on the "big case."

GRACE

I've really been trying to assess this case objectively, as I think I always do, but you know, Gabe... I wish I wasn't bracing myself for another Constitutional protection case that will end up trying to rely on precedence rulings for a defense.

GABRIELLE

Realizing full well, that Dad probably wrote some of those precedence rulings.

GRACE

The Constitution and the Bill of Rights are among the most well-respected and intuitive documents in American culture. Their mere existence creates a legal and moral framework by which both I and the jury must operate within. Unfortunately, the legal system currently has no shortage of fast-thinking, constitutionally-savvy defense attorneys who improperly bend and twist these documents, with the end result intended to be a safe haven and a justification for defending their clients' illegal activities. But having said that, I still ardently support the form and functionality of these great pieces of legislation.

GABRIELLE

Well, what I think understand about the law, is
that you are supposed to take precedence rulings
into consideration if the facts are similar,
right?

GRACE

Well, if the previous findings are comparable to
those being tried and the defense can argue
those similarities, precedence rulings are
frequently upheld. It is up to the prosecution
to uncover some tangible, meaningful difference
that would override the precedence ruling.

GABRIELLE

Sometimes difficult but not impossible, right?

GRACE

Right. I cannot allow this ruling to be
appealed and overruled, I'll be the
laughingstock of the circuit. I'm still
considered a "rookie" and two of my last three
rulings were appealed. You know how important
this seat is to me, I've worked so hard to get
to this stage in my career!

GABRIELLE

Though we may only be separated by four years,
that's another area of life where we are so
totally different!

GRACE

How so?

GABRIELLE

You identify your success in life with the success of your career! Your seat as a judge!

GRACE

It's an appointment of many challenges and rewards!

GABRIELLE

I measure the successes in my life by the help I give to others and also, what they bring to me.

(pauses for effect)

You never mention the people, those that operate within that circle or those of us who don't. All work and no play make Gracie a boring and might I add, a very lonely gal!

GRACE

Wrong, Gabe! You've got it all wrong, from a personal standpoint anyway. However, you are 100% correct in observing that I can't allow emotion to influence my professional life. My sentence in this case must be based on the evidence and the facts.

GABRIELLE

So there's our Gracie...

> (holding her arms out to each side
> as if tipping the scales of
> justice)

Weighing in on the scales of justice, trying to
make sure both sides are equal.

> (laughing)

A little bit of uncertainty, a little bit of
self-righteousness, a lot of faith in a
sometimes failing legal system... In other
words, you're walking the old buffet...of
emotions, remember?

GRACE

Buffet?

> (said puzzled and then cracks up
> laughing)

My God, I haven't heard you use that expression
in years...the old buff-ette of emotions, why...
that's it!!!

> (still laughing)

GABRIELLE

Little sister ought to hang her shingle out
right next to Mitch the shrinks! I have SOOO
missed my calling!

> (pauses for effect)

So you're saying that you will somehow be able
to legally and morally rationalize a not guilty
verdict if this sleaze bag gets off the hook?

GRACE

If the evidence presented supports it and the
precedence can support it and the jury rules
accordingly, then yes, that's exactly what I'm
saying!

GABRIELLE

I guess I just don't see how the cold, hard
truth isn't sometimes more persuasive and
convincing in this case... And I know we can't
discuss the details.

GRACE

No, we can't! And I guess all I can say is that
the cold, hard truth can be ugly and painful and
sad...but the law is the law!

GABRIELLE

(shrugging her shoulders and
motioning with her hands, as if
to say, "you win")

Drink up, big sister. We're supposed to be
having fun tonight, not pondering the meaning of
the fabric that holds our nation together.

GRACE

Sorry, Gabe, you're right!

> (taking a big chug of her Martini
> and popping an olive into her
> mouth)

So what's new in your life, sweetie?

> (reaching over and ruffling her
> little sister's hair)

GABRIELLE

Well, I've had a couple of recent success
stories at the center

> (said with a twinkle in her eye as
> she starts to explain)

Remember Richard, the severely disabled boy that
I was shooting hoops with the last time you were
in?

GRACE

Yes, of course I remember!

GABRIELLE

He is actually going to get a spot on the
Special Olympics team. He is so proud! His
Mother actually broke down, thanking me for my
patience and hard work!

                          GRACE

              (clapping her hands together and
                taking a sip of her Martini)

Bravo, little sister! You're an inspiration!

                        GABRIELLE

Well, this inspirational little sister has an
early start ahead of me for tomorrow, so let's
continue this conversation next time!

                    The sisters get up and exit.

                                        CUT TO:

II.6 INT. THE COURTROOM - MORNING

                    *The bailiff enters. Shouting
                    and protesting can be heard
                    outside.*

                         BAILIFF

All rise, the Honorable Grace Porter presiding.

                    *Grace enters the courtroom,
                    takes her seat and POUNDS the
                    gavel.*

                          GRACE

Please be seated. Court is now in session.
Deliberations for the people of the Commonwealth
of Virginia, versus Noah Lester, d/b/a Noah's
ARK will continue. Mr. Pantovere, I believe you

are going to continue with presenting the
commonwealth's evidence?

                    PANTOVERE

That is correct, your Honor!

                      GRACE

Continue, please!

                    PANTOVERE

Ladies and gentlemen of the jury, the violence
that occurred in Charlottesville on August 12,
2017, was in no way the result of a rally that
got out of hand. There was a very concerted
effort among Mr. Lester and other members of
alt-right establishments to collaborate,
disseminate, willfully plan and encourage
violence! In the months and weeks prior to
August 12, 2017, Mr. Lester on his web site and
other social media platforms, posted articles
and other propaganda in support of the "Unite
The Right" rally, including establishing a
"Charlottesville 2.0" server on Discord to
secretly plan acts of violence among the inner
circle of top ranking members, including
promotional materials and posters, some of which
are included in the commonwealth's exhibits to
follow.

          (pauses)

Unfortunately, continued advances in technology
and in social media platforms provide a
mechanism for secret communications that can be

used for illegal activities and also for
misinformation to be widely distributed to
targeted audiences, as we have repeatedly been
made aware of since Russia's interference in our
2016 election.

(pauses for effect)

I hope that the CEOs and senior leadership of
these mega corporations start to realize the
harmful effects that can be a direct result of
their social media platforms being ill used for
deviant activities. However, this is one for
instance, when our ability to capture these
written messages and instructions has been
instrumental in our ability to bring charges
against the accused.

(pauses for effect)

In their months of preparation for the
Charlottesville rally, the eager white
supremacists stated that, "We are stepping off
the internet in a big way..." "I'm ready to
crack skulls." Some of the leaders encouraged
bringing concealed and non-concealed weapons,
while other leaders advised not to carry
anything that's, ..."explicitly a weapon." The
intention to engage in violence was openly
communicated and explicit. Ladies and gentlemen
of the jury, let me share with you two of the
posters that were widely distributed prior to
August 12, 2017, which include the official
"Unite The Right" Rally poster and another
poster, holding a dagger, dripping in blood,
which reads, "Fight Until The Last Drop." I
present these as Exhibits "B" and "C."

> *Pantovere hands the two*
> *posters to the bailiff.*

PANTOVERE (CONT'D)

I agree with you! There leaves nothing to the
imagination regarding the intentions of the
white supremacist protesters on that day. A look
out was stationed across the street from the
Walker's home to advise Mr. Lester of their
departure the day of the rally so that he could
monitor their location. Protesters arrived at
Lee park that morning in groups to intimidate
and terrorize the citizens of Charlottesville
who were peacefully protesting along with
members of other groups, including Antifa.
According to the Police Chief, the white
supremacists failed to follow the plan that had
been arranged to keep them separated from the
counter-protesters, swarming the park from all
sides, with an estimated 80% being armed with
semiautomatic weapons, shouting racial slurs
like, "Hitler did nothing wrong."

SNAYDER

Your Honor, objection! No one is suggesting
that this court or the jury or anyone else for
that matter approve of the aforementioned
examples of the written or spoken word. My
client and his membership have the right to
express their viewpoints. Your aversion does
not override their right to expression. Let's
face it, there is no way that over two hundred
years ago, the founders could have ever imagined
technological advances such as the internet.
Thomas Jefferson himself referred to the
Constitution as a "living document." To quote
the late, great Alexander Hamilton, he said
that, "Freedom consists in the right to publish,
with impunity, truth, with good motives, for
justifiable ends." We are not asking or

expecting that you share the ideologies of white supremacist groups. Whether you like it or not, their First Amendment rights have repeatedly been upheld.

                                    CUT TO: CLOSE ON

II.7 INT. THE RED ROOM - SAME TIME

>   *Washington, Hamilton,*
>   *Jefferson and Franklin are*
>   *sitting or standing around*
>   *the room intently watching*
>   *these courtroom proceedings.*

                    ALEXANDER HAMILTON

I did say that, freedom consists in the right to publish, with impunity, truth, with good motives, for justifiable ends, but how in all of the heavens could counsel suggest to a courtroom of peers and authority alike that these ends could be construed as justifiable or that the motives were good? The ends must justify the means!

                        THOMAS JEFFERSON

For once I agree with you, Alexander! **This was not what we had in mind!** That was my concern all along... My desire has been to see a declaration that the federal government will never restrain the presses from printing anything they please, but will not take away the liability of the printers for false facts printed.

GEORGE WASHINGTON

It is safe to say, that the passage of time will
never eliminate the nagging journalistic
contributions of infamous scribblers, whose
opinions are an unwelcome but necessary
nuisance.

> *Show Benjamin Franklin*
> *walking around the room and*
> *stops to tip up a lamp shade*
> *and looks at the light bulb.*

BENJAMIN FRANKLIN

A miraculous scientific breakthrough, if I do
say so myself!

> (chuckling to himself and then
> speaking with great conviction)

I say take the cudgels and break the
rapscallions head. We need laws to govern the
presses, gentlemen, let us not confuse freedom
and individual liberties with anarchy.

CUT TO:

II.8 INT. BACK TO COURT ROOM - SAME TIME

GRACE

Mr. Pantovere, continue please.

84

PANTOVERE

Your Honor, I need to provide several more
examples of the specific instructions Mr. Lester
was broadcasting to the driver of the car, Alan
Shields, as pandemonium broke out during the
Charlottesville "Unite the Right" rally. As I
mentioned previously, Mr. Lester had a lookout
monitoring the Walker family's home the morning
of August 12 and at roughly 9:00AM he sent a
text message to Mr. Shields and others
advising,"Kiked-up nigger family leaving their
house and on their way to meet up with other
counter-protesters, stay clear for further
instructions." At 10:00AM Lester texted,
"They're on their way to Emancipation Park with
the other Jews and Commies, rev your engines!"
At 11:22AM Lester texted, problems at EP,
Charlottesville faggot cops stepping in and
interfering with our God ordained plans, crowd
dispersing, along with Walkers, still in our
sights, will likely need to modify location for
the "ultimate destruction." At 11:28 AM former
Governor McAuliffe declaring SOS regroup and
redirect to McIntire Park immediately! At
1:08PM everyone started getting kicked out of
McIntire Park.

(pauses for effect)

Many of the peaceful protesters, including the
Walker family proceeded to the pedestrian mall.
All hell was breaking loose everywhere. Local
law enforcement underestimated the magnitude of
violence that erupted and were unprepared.
There was no peaceful protesting being allowed
because violence, bigotry and hatred were
everywhere! Mr. Lester than texted, "The time
is now, claim your glory and victory, the Walker

family are sitting ducks, hit the accelerator"
At 1:40PM, Alan Shields drove his Dodge
Challenger into a crowd of peaceful protesters,
killing three members of the Walker family and
injuring over thirty others. By 2:25PM that
afternoon, the defendant and other members of
his alt-right groups realized that the situation
was out of control and started ordering everyone
to get out of town! Later that evening, after
the reality of the magnitude of the carnage set
in and was being broadcast around the world, Mr.
Lester and others shared the message, "At least
nobody important got hurt," and "THE STREET WAR
HAS ENDED. WE WON. WE SHOWED THAT OUR IDEAS
HAVE TO BE SHUT DOWN WITH VIOLENCE," and "Dirty
Apes playing in the street gotta learn the hard
way."

(pauses for effect)

I have two children, your Honor. Mr. Lester's
words and actions speak for themselves.

GRACE

Mr. Pantovere, are you just about finished?

PANTOVERE

Yes, your Honor! I would like to conclude today
by again stating that First Amendment protection
is not an absolute. The finding of American
Communications Ass'n, C.I.O. v. Douds reveals
that the Constitution permits limitations on
"speech which advocates conduct inimical to the
public welfare." The safety of the citizens of
Charlottesville on August 12 was obviously a
significant public welfare interest. Lastly, in

Brandenburg v. Ohio, the Supreme Court established the more contemporary "clear and present danger" doctrine, ruling that speech that is, "directed to inciting or producing imminent lawless action, and is likely to incite or produce such action," is not protected by the First Amendment.

GRACE

Well said and thank you, Mr. Pantovere. Mr. Snadyer, do you have anything you would like to add as we conclude for the day?

SNAYDER

Yes, your Honor, in closing, I just want to reiterate that this great country gives us the privilege of choosing chocolate or vanilla, so even if you do not like the flavor by which my client chooses to make his living, or the manner by which he chooses to express his thoughts and ideologies, or the company he keeps, that does not mean that you can persecute him for doing so. As stated in Metromedia, Inc., V. City of San Diego, "democracy stands on a stronger footing when courts protect First Amendment interests, against legislative intrusions rather than deferring to merely rational legislative judgments in this area." Thank you, ladies and gentlemen of the jury. I have nothing further today.

GRACE

That will conclude our session for the day. Court is adjourned until Monday.

Grace POUNDS the gavel.

            BAILIFF

All rise....

      *Grace stands and exits the
      courtroom. The attorneys
      gather their paperwork and
      close their briefcases as
      they stand and walk out of
      the court room.*

      *In departing, Snayder SLAPS
      his client on the back and
      they walk out of the
      courtroom together.*

            SNAYDER

Don't worry, Lester, I have a trump card or two
to play next round!

                      CUT TO:

ACT III

CLARITY

III.1 INT. GRACE'S TOWNHOUSE - NIGHT

> *Gabrielle enters and sets down her overnight bag. The sisters exchange a quick hug and a kiss.*

GRACE

It's been so long since we had a sister sleep over! What are we going to binge watch on Netflix?

GABRIELLE

I was surprised to hear from you this afternoon. I guess I'm feeling a little sorry for Mitch's sake that you'd rather spend your Friday night with me versus him, but hey, it's your call! What did you get to eat? I'm starving?

GRACE

You know that's the one thing I didn't have time to pick up, so we'll order some take out! Somewhere that delivers nearby!

GABRIELLE

Oh, I know of this great new Italian place
that's pretty close to here. The guy that
usually delivers is H-O-T, HOT! I know you
can't talk much about it, but it sounds like
you're in the hot seat, with the Charlottesville
case!

GRACE

Well no, I can't say much of anything about it,
but this case is certainly taking up a lot of my
time, so I'm glad we could get together and just
kick back for an evening. I have a pitcher of
Margaritas in the freezer and a blender full of
"the eternal fountain of youth," so pull your
hair back and we'll officially kick off "girl's
night."

> Grace pours a Margarita for
> Gabe and hands her a bowl of
> a DIY face mask and a roll of
> paper towels, as they take
> turns applying the facial
> mask.

GRACE (CONT'D)

OK, we've got plain yogurt, honey, almond oil,
coconut oil and all kinds of other goodies in
here to pamper and refresh our weary
complexions.

> The girls take turns rubbing
> the concoction on their
> faces.

GABRIELLE

Wow, it's a little messy! Sheet masks would have probably been a lot easier!

(laughing)

GRACE

Hey, the blog post says this will make your skin glowing and refreshed.

GABRIELLE

How long do we have to leave this stuff on?

GRACE

Oh, twenty-thirty minutes.

The two women touch their faces to check on the "beautifying mask."

GABRIELLE

I'm calling for food, Gracie! I'm ravished! Is Italian all right for you?

GRACE

Fine with me.

Gabrielle grabs her cell phone from her purse and dials.

GABRIELLE

(into phone)

OK, we'd like one order of Vegetable Lasagna,
one order of Angel Hair Chicken Pasta and one
order of Eggplant Parmesan, with a large salad
and lots of bread for delivery. Yes, it's 6775
Montrose Avenue. Is A.J. delivering tonight?
Great, great, I'll be looking forward to it!

> *Gabrielle starts to head for
> the bathroom.*

GRACE

Where are you going, Gabe? Time's not up yet.

GABRIELLE

Yeah, speak for yourself, sister, who has an
incredible hunk-o-man in her life. I'm washing
this fruit salad off of my face before my date
with destiny arrives.

GRACE

Gabe, he's delivering dinner. We get to spend
the evening reminiscing and hanging out. I've
had a really stressful week and I've been
looking forward to it!

> *The doorbell RINGS and
> Gabrielle heads toward the
> door to answer it.*

GABRIELLE

(yelling over her shoulder)

I'll get the door

(primping her hair)

Destiny is waiting!

> *She opens the door to find*
> *the handsome A.J. standing*
> *there with their food.*

GABRIELLE (CONT'D)

Aah... A.J.

(taking the food from him)

So good to see you again!

(she gives him a kiss on each
cheek)

My sister and I were just catching up and I was
getting ready to leave.

(flirtatiously, touches his
shoulder)

When, you gorgeous thing, may I ask... Do you
"get off?"

(coyly)

> *Grace watches this*
> *flirtatious exchange and is*
> *getting uncomfortable with*
> *her sister's forwardness.*

*Grace walks up to the door.
Oblivious to the fact that
the facial mask is still on.*

GRACE

Hi, I'm Grace Porter, Gabrielle's sister.

(shaking his hand)

What do we owe you this evening, A.J.?

A.J.

$58.50

GRACE

Great, here you go.

(hands him several bills)

Please keep the change. We are two hungry gals.
Everything smells fabulous!

GABRIELLE

So, is this your last delivery tonight?

*Still flirtatious and
starting to caress his
shoulder and arm.*

A.J.

(openly affectionate as well)

Well, it could be!

> *Gabrielle walks across the
> room to gather her overnight
> bag and returns to A.J.'s
> Side, and he puts his arm
> around Gabrielle's shoulder.*

GABRIELLE

Gracie, it's been great catching up, but I'm
quite sure you'll have just as good of a time
without me, relaxing and having your spa night.

> *Gabrielle puts her arm around
> A.J. and they turn to exit
> out the door.*

> *Grace, in her exasperation,
> follows Gabrielle and grabs
> her arm to pull her back into
> the house.*

GRACE

(said half angrily/half
protectively)

Gabrielle, what do you think you're doing?
Where are you going? We were just starting to
have fun!

GABRIELLE

It's been a blast, Grace... I've just decided
there's been a change in plans, that's all.

>   (kisses her sister and hugs her
>   affectionately)

Enjoy your binge watching. I'll call you. Not
for nothing but you are sexy as hell in that
face mask!

>   (said jokingly)

                    GRACE

Gabrielle... You can't... You don't know what
you're doing... come back...

                    GABRIELLE

>   (cutting her sister off mid
>   sentence)

Stop, Grace. You're embarrassing me. I'm too
old for the twenty questions routine. Good
night.

                    GRACE

>   (pulling her sister aside)

I'm embarrassing you? You're embarrassing me!

                    GABRIELLE

Why can't you be as open-minded of a sister as
you are a judge? Just let me go like you do all
of the babbling freaks and lunatics! After all,
I'm just exercising my constitutional right to
do whatever I damn well please!

                    GRACE

No matter who it hurts?

                  GABRIELLE

Think about that for a minute, Grace. I'll talk
to you soon. Go enjoy dinner.

                         Gabrielle walks away with her
                         arm around A.J. Grace closes
                         the door behind her and leans
                         against the wall with a thud.

                    GRACE

I can't believe my little sister just picked up
the delivery man!

Ugh... My sister... The Ho!

                         Grace plops herself down on
                         the couch, still wearing the
                         mask on her face, opens up
                         the bag of takeout food and
                         starts to read her "gift
                         book."

                                    CUT TO:

III.2 INT. THE COURTROOM - MORNING

                         The bailiff enters the
                         courtroom. Shouting and
                         protesting can be heard
                         outside the doors.

BAILIFF

All rise, the Honorable Grace Porter presiding.

*Grace enters the courtroom
and takes her seat and POUNDS
the gavel.*

GRACE

Please be seated. Court is now in session. Mr.
Snayder are you prepared to present the defense
on behalf of Mr. Lester?

SNAYDER

Yes, your Honor. I have been listening to Mr.
Pantovere with great interest. It is
coincidental that one of the charges, also
currently being brought against my client, Noah
Lester, in a separate civil case, is in
violating The Civil Rights Act of 1871, a/k/a
The Ku Klux Klan Act.

(pauses for effect)

As I have already stated, no one in this court
room here today needs to share my client's
beliefs, neither the words he speaks with his
members or the communications that he writes via
his website or other social media platforms. We
all have the option of tuning out versus tuning
in. It's as simple as that!

(pauses for effect)

But since our current legal system allows for
these charges, stemming from a decision dating
back to 1871, I would like to share with you,

ladies and gentlemen of the jury, a great and
important case in this country's history. John
Peter Zenger was charged with seditious libel in
1735 as a result of his papers publishing what
was considered, at that time, to be inflammatory
statements against the Governor of New York,
William Crosby. Zenger's brilliant defense
attorney, Alexander Hamilton, argued the
necessity of truth being used as a defense and
that the jury would decide the criminality of
his actions.

(pauses for effect)

Prior to this occasion, and even sometimes
afterwards, the charge of seditious libel was
interpreted with a common law meaning and was
considered to be enough, in and of itself, to
accuse a man, without trial by jury, and was
punishable by death. Luckily, for John Peter
Zenger, that was not the case and ultimately,
the jury acquitted Zenger and he was, indeed, a
free man.

(pauses for effect)

Mr. Lester has built a considerable reputation
over the years and is viewed by his membership
to share articles of great "journalistic
integrity," which the great framers went to
great pains to protect via the First Amendment.

PANTOVERE

(stands up and is looking
extremely agitated)

So, let me get this straight... you are, in
effect, comparing the trial of a publisher

accused of printing inevitably true statements
of a political nature, to a charge of aiding and
abetting in murder, by a hate-incited rally of
an army of white supremacists? Where the
defendant's explicit instructions via multiple
social media platforms, led to the murder of a
mother and her two children by one of these
protesters who executed upon these said
instructions by driving into them with his car?

(getting loud and angry)

Am I correct in understanding the parallel you
are drawing for us here today in this court
room, Mr. Snayder?

SNAYDER

You are correct. It nevertheless, draws a
parallel regarding the public's critical
endorsement of protecting the, "right to
publish... with impunity...

PANTOVERE

(visibly agitated)

Your Honor, have you ever heard of such an
unlikely attempt to draw a parallel or
precedence ruling?

(laughing)

Hellooo...hellooo

(rapping the side of his head with
the heel of his hand, there is
laughter in the court room)

Is anybody home? Clearly, you are sorely
lacking for any type of legitimate defense to
even attempt to use such a far-fetched,
antiquated example!

                    SNAYDER

Your Honor, I ask that last exchange be stricken
from the record. Counsel, again, is trying to
color the jury's opinion!

                    GRACE

Sustained! It is a far stretch to my
understanding as well, but watch your wording,
Mr. Pantovere!

                   PANTOVERE

And one more thing... I wasn't aware that the
defendant, Noah Lester, had a literary
reputation which would classify him as a
"journalist," and I am relatively confident that
if James Madison, George Washington or any one
of the great framers of The Bill of Rights were
present in this courtroom today... Mr. Lester
would not be their poster boy for ratification!

                    *There is great LAUGHTER in
                    the courtroom!*

                    GRACE

              (with an aggravated tone)

Very amusing, Mr. Pantovere. Mr. Snayder,
continue.

SNAYDER

Thank you, your Honor. Now as I was saying,
until I got so rudely interrupted...

(glaring at Pantovere)

Mr. Pantovere, in one of your earlier arguments,
you stated that the framers of the Constitution
and the Bill of Rights intent, was to apply the
laws as appropriate at that time, that every
possible scenario could not be foreseen and that
we have the benefit of "interpretive latitude."

PANTOVERE

Objection, your Honor! My argument for the
necessity for "interpretive latitude" was not
intended to be interpreted by defense counsel as
a far-fetched, self-serving attempt to create
precedence!

CUT TO: CLOSE ON

III.3 INT. THE RED ROOM - SAME TIME

> *John Adams and Alexander
> Hamilton are watching the
> courtroom proceedings and
> engaged in conversation.*

JOHN ADAMS

It certainly seems as if these instances of
precedence rulings weigh heavily on the ultimate
verdict. Facts are stubborn things, and
whatever may be our wishes, our inclinations, or

the dictates of our passions, they cannot alter the state of facts and evidence.

ALEXANDER HAMILTON

I must say, I steadfastly agree with the prosecutions questioning defense counsel's appropriateness of using the Zenger case.

(said as an aside)

After all... I was there!

(chuckling)

Hellooo...hellooo

(rapping the heel of his hand on his head)

Is anybody home? Why, I think I quite appreciate Mr. Pantovere's witty and humorous response!

CUT TO:

III.4 INT. BACK TO COURT ROOM - SAME TIME

GRACE

Sustained! Where are you going with this, Mr. Snayder?

SNAYDER

I am simply trying to impress upon the jury that if they are to be the judges in determining whether First Amendment protection is applicable and you are arguing that such a protection is not available in light of the "intent" of the written word, that it is only fair that the jury be given other examples of how our laws were interpreted during our country's nascency and of the significance placed on the liberties that we now recognize as being protected. Your Honor, let me also share with the ladies and gentlemen of the jury, some high-profile cases citing the critical nature of First Amendment protection. To quote the late, great Supreme Court Justice Norman John Porter...

                    GRACE

           (interrupting him mid-sentence)

I know where you're going with this, counselor and I DO NOT like it! You are treading on thin ice, so I warn you to proceed with caution!

                   SNAYDER

To continue...

              (pauses for effect)

Justice Porter, whose rulings I am sure you are quite familiar with...

              (pauses for effect)

Judge Porter..., found in Brandenburg v. Ohio, that, an Ohio criminal statute was unconstitutional because the statute broadly prohibited the mere advocacy of violence. A finding which resulted in one other Supreme

Court decision being overruled and casting doubt
on several others.

(pauses for effect)

This is the perfect narrative for the events at
Charlottesville and the written and spoken words
of my client.

(pauses for effect)

Furthermore, quite recently, our very own Judge
Grace Porter here presided over a not guilty
finding on all counts for the first six
defendants tried in the J20 hearings, charged
with felony rioting charges during inauguration
day of President Trump and his administration.
I am aghast at how inappropriately my client has
been charged, when the law seems to side quite
differently with others facing similar charges.

CUT TO:

III.5 INT. THE RED ROOM - SAME TIME

> *George Washington is intently
> viewing the courtroom
> proceedings with great
> interest.*

GEORGE WASHINGTON

Laws made by common consent must not be trampled
on by individuals. I quite agree with Justice
Porter's statement that one of the fundamental
purposes of free speech is to invite dispute,
even to the point of anger. But defense counsel
and his client, Lester, are taking this too far!
We're talking about the demise of a young

family! Mr. Lester's counsel is craftily
attempting to create a plausible argument, plant
a seed of reasonable doubt, so that his client
may continue with his diabolical and hate-filled
ideological agenda.

CUT TO:

III.6 INT. BACK TO COURT ROOM - SAME TIME

GRACE

Mr. Snayder, are you quite through with the
barrage of inapplicable Supreme Court rulings by
my late Father and me?

(visibly agitated)

It is not me, that you ultimately have to
convince, it is the jury! But since we have
been obliged to listen to your never ending
diatribe of precedence rulings, let me share
with this courtroom, that none of those
precedence rulings are an appropriate defense
for a charge of aiding and abetting in a murder
or murders. Mr. Pantovere, would you like to
respond to Mr. Snayder's most recent assertions
of precedence rulings here? It is really not my
place to be making such determinations, it is
yours.

MICHAEL PANTOVERE

Certainly, your Honor. I have already
introduced the Supreme Court's ruling for
Brandenburg, the Court held that government
cannot punish inflammatory speech unless that
speech is directed to inciting or producing

imminent lawless action, which is certainly the
case in these current proceedings. So you left
that part out, Mr. Snayder. You need to bring
your "A game" when you're up against me!

(pauses for effect)

In regard to your recent J20 case, it was a
surprise to many of us in the legal system that
those charges were actually allowed to be filed
in the first place. Of the over 200 protesters
that were arrested and charged, only about 20
individuals or roughly 10% actually were
convicted. There was zero evidence that the
other 90% did anything wrong whatsoever. So
that was a perfect example of an egregious waste
of taxpayers' money and not at all the situation
that unfolded during the Charlottesville rally!
The murder, violence, chaos and destruction were
televised for the whole world to see!
Atrocities that were premeditated and
orchestrated well in advance!

                    GRACE

Thank you, Mr. Pantovere. Are you finished, Mr.
Snyder?

                    SNAYDER

No, your Honor, I have a witness ready to call
to the stand.

                    GRACE

Proceed!

SNAYDER

The defense calls Spencer Matthew to the stand.

> *Spencer Matthew, a red-neck,*
> *hillbilly sounding white*
> *supremacist takes the stand*
> *and holds up his right hand.*

BAILIFF

Spencer Matthew, do you swear to tell the truth, the whole truth and nothing but the truth, so help you God?

SPENCER MATTHEW

I do!

GRACE

So sworn, please proceed, Mr. Snayder

SNAYDER

Mr. Matthew how do you know the defendant, Noah Lester?

SPENCER MATTHEW

I am a privileged member of the Alt-Right Knights, we call us Noah's ARK. Noah Lester is our leader, we look to him like the Noah of biblical prophecy leading us to safety and to the promised land, where we will be acknowledged as supreme rulers in a country with brothers of like colors and religions.

PANTOVERE

(stands up agitated)

Right, except this is 2019, 156 years after the Emancipation Proclamation was issued by Abraham Lincoln. The 13th Amendment was passed in 1865, which abolished slavery, the 14th Amendment was passed in 1868, which provided black people with citizenship and equal protection of the law and the 15th Amendment, which was passed in 1870, gave our black citizens the right to vote. In 1954 Brown v. Board of Education was passed in the Supreme Court and finally overturned the "separate but equal" doctrine advanced in Plessy v. Ferguson. The Jim Crow Laws were abolished by President Lyndon Johnson when he signed the Civil Rights Act of 1964. The country that you aspire to live in was declared unconstitutional over a hundred years ago!

SNAYDER

Objection!

GRACE

Sustained! Mr. Pantovere, zip it! You'll get your chance to cross!

SNAYDER

Thank you. Were you in attendance at the "Unite the Right" rally in Charlottesville, VA the weekend of August 11-12, 2017?

SPENCER MATTHEW

Yes sir, I proudly was there!

SNAYDER

Were you there at the urging of Mr. Lester?

SPENCER MATTHEW

Yes sir, I was, along with many other members of our society.

SNAYDER

Did you attend the "Unite the Right" rally in Emancipation Park on August 12th, 2017 in Charlottesville, VA and were you receiving text messages and other social media messages from Mr. Lester and other alt-right group leaders throughout your attendance at the rally?

SPENCER MATTHEW

Yes sir, helped to keep us united!

                    SNAYDER

And to confirm...Mr. Lester also urged you to
drive your vehicle into a crowd of peaceful
protesters, did he not?

                 SPENCER MATTHEW

Yes sir, he did!

                    SNAYDER

And why did you decide to not follow the orders
of your leader?

                 SPENCER MATTHEW

Well, I thought good and hard about it, cause I
really hate them Jews, niggers and queers...

                     GRACE

          (Visibly exasperated and cutting
            him off mid sentence)

Oh, for the love of...

          (trying to control her anger)

How about I call you an out of touch,
uneducated, racist, foul-mouthed red neck?

          (regaining her composure)

Ladies and gentlemen of the jury, counsel, I
have to draw the line somewhere! I will not

have that language in my courtroom! Mr.
Snayder, please proceed with questioning.

                    SNAYDER

Please continue Mr. Matthew. My apologies for
the interruption!

                SPENCER MATTHEW

Well, my wife and me just had my little baby
boy, whom I respectfully named, Noah Matthew,
after our great leader and I guess I kept
thinkin that if something happened and I ended
up going to jail, my baby boy wouldn't have a
Daddy for a while, so I guess that tempered my
actions.

                    SNAYDER

So, despite the fact that you were ordered to do
so, your conscience stopped you from doing so?

                SPENCER MATTHEW

Yes sir, I guess that's so, but I am sorry for
letting my leader, Noah Lester, down.

                    SNAYDER

OK, so ladies and gentlemen of the jury, there
you have it. Mr. Matthew was given the same
instructions as Alan Shields on August 12th in
Charlottesville but he chose to refrain from
carrying out those instructions because HIS
conscience dictated him to do so. There you

have it, Mr. Lester gave the same instructions
to two of his followers, one of them complied
and the other one didn't. So, it wasn't Mr.
Lester's instructions that were the problem, it
was Mr. Shield's response to them. The blame
rests on Mr. Shields not my client. Ladies and
gentlemen of the jury, this should be proof that
it is an individual's own thought processes that
lead them to react to instructions or directions
differently. My client is innocent of the
charges against him!

(pauses for effect)

I have one last comment, your Honor...

(said with great pomp and
circumstance)

In our constitutional system of government we
are free because the government is not; the
government is not free because of the
limitations imposed upon it by the Constitution,
including the Bill of Rights.

GRACE

Mr. Pantovere, your volley.

PANTOVERE

Let me conclude, your Honor, by advising the
jury that, Political **LIBERTY** consists in a
freedom of speech and action, so far as the laws
of a community will permit, and no farther; all
beyond is criminal and tend to the destruction
of **LIBERTY** itself.

(pauses for effect)

I have nothing to cross this witness on because I don't even understand the argument that is being made here! Are we supposed to be impressed because he didn't RAM his car into a group of peaceful protesters because he has a baby now? The same guy who views the defendant as some type of prophet? Where are we going to draw the line? White supremacists have no place in our country!

(pauses for effect)

I urge this court and... this country to re-examine and encourage a rediscovery, why... A renaissance of the laws and the documents that serve as the foundation of this country and to recognize...

(pauses for effect)

Just how far we have strayed!

CUT TO:

III.7 INT. THE RED ROOM - SAME TIME

Thomas Jefferson is watching the courtroom proceedings with great interest.

THOMAS JEFFERSON

(Said thoughtfully and with great introspection)

LIBERTY is the capacity to do anything that does no harm to others. The care of every man's soul belongs to himself. But what if he neglects the care of his health or his estate...? Will the magistrate make a law that he shall not be poor or sick? **Laws provide against injury from others, but not from ourselves. God himself will not save men against their wills.**

CUT TO:

III.8 INT. GRACE'S OFFICE - MORNING

Grace walks into her office as her cell phone RINGS.

GRACE

(speaking into the phone to Mitch)

Hey, there! Great timing, I was just going to shoot you a quick text because I just had to share with you something that happened in court this afternoon, which I am able to broadly discuss.

MITCH

(v.o)

Let's hear it!

GRACE

The defense attorney attempted to use precedence rulings from both my Father and I and it literally blew up in his face!

MITCH

(v.o)

LOL! Tell me more!

GRACE

He tried to use the Brandenburg ruling from my
father and then tried to use the J20 findings in
his favor. Too much! Trying to say that
because almost all of the J20 protesters were
found innocent of felonious rioting and
incitement to violence that his white
supremacist client's Charlottesville attacks
should also be vindicated.

MITCH

(v.o)

At least some of the checks and balances seem to
be working as they were meant to be.

GRACE

I'm still amazed that most people never heard
about the J20 arrests and charges to begin with!

MITCH

(v.o)

If more than a handful had been convicted, it
would have been all over the news! How about
dinner tonight?

                    GRACE

Ugh, Mitch, I just can't. You know I'm right in
the middle of this trial and I just can't seem
to find enough hours in the day.

                    MITCH

                 (v.o)

Damn it Grace! When do I... I mean we, ever
come first? If you can't seem to find time for
us anymore, just say the word and I won't bother
you anymore.

                    GRACE

Mitch, please!

                    MITCH

                 (v.o)

No more, "Mitch please!" Grace, I've had it!
Do you think that I don't have an equally hectic
schedule? Do you, Grace? I am just so tired of
your shit!

                    GRACE

Mitch, stop it...please!

                 (she breaks down and starts to cry)

No more, I can't... My shit, your shit...that's
a lot of shit!

(laughing through her sobs)

MITCH

(v.o)

Grace, sweetheart, I didn't mean to make you
cry. I'm sorry. This trial has really gotten
to you, I've never heard you sound so
overwhelmed. I'm sorry. How can I help?

GRACE

No, I'm the one who should be saying I'm
sorry... And I am. You're right, I have been a
selfish, self-absorbed, pain in the ass. Dinner
would be great, thank you for asking me.

MITCH

(v.o)

Why don't you come over around 7 or so? I'll
have Tucker whip us up something.

GRACE

Oh no, don't go to any trouble. Why don't we
just go out somewhere?

MITCH

(v.o)

It's no trouble, I insist!

GRACE

OK then, sounds great.

(sniffling)

I'll see you tonight.

MITCH

(v.o)

I'm looking forward to it. Are you OK?

GRACE

Yes, fine, I guess.

(sniffling)

See you then.

> *Grace hangs up the phone and sits at her desk with her head in her hands for a minute. She then sits down on the sofa in her office and reads her "gift book" for a few minutes before sitting back down at her desk and picks up the phone, dialing her sister.*

GRACE (CONT'D)

(Speaking into the phone to Gabrielle)

Gabrielle! Glad I caught you. How's the best little sister in the whole world?

                    GABRIELLE

                     (v.o)

I figured you'd still be pissed off at me for my... Indiscretions.

                     GRACE

Not pissed off, just concerned for your well-being. That being said, I hope your evening lived up to your expectations.

                    GABRIELLE

                     (v.o)

Far exceeded! And thanks for asking! Better than sitting around with my old bat of a sister talking about the good ole days!

                     GRACE

Old bat? Just wait a few years Gabe. It'll be like looking in the mirror.

                    GABRIELLE

                     (v.o)

Probably so, Gracie. What's on your mind?

GRACE

Nothing special. Just wanted to talk. How's
your day going?

GABRIELLE

(v.o)

Off to a good start so far. You sound awfully
happy, tell me, who's the culprit?

GRACE

Well, Mitch, I guess! Hot date tonight!

GABRIELLE

(v.o)

Really? Scoop me!

GRACE

Well, Mitch and I had a little "tiff" on the
phone earlier, so we're going to get together
tonight and patch things up.

GABRIELLE

(v.o)

Well, I'm dying for you two to kiss and make up
too. Where is this little rendezvous taking
place?

GRACE

Mitch's.

GABRIELLE

(v.o)

Aah, sounds perfect. Of course, I'll need the details. Call me tomorrow as soon as you can or I'll come and find you.

GRACE

I'm not going to give you all the details, but I'll share some of the more memorable "highlights."

GABRIELLE

(v.o)

Well, if that's the best you can do, I'll look forward to it. Have a good time, Grace. You two deserve it. Love you.

GRACE

I love you too! We'll talk tomorrow.

> Grace grabs her "gift book" and sits down on her sofa to read for a while, glancing at her watch, from time to time. Finally Grace grabs her briefcase and exits.

CUT TO:

III.9 INT. MITCH'S HOUSE/DINING ROOM - EVENING

> *Grace enters and hands Mitch a bottle of wine.*

MITCH

Right on time and lovely as always.

> *They embrace/kiss.*

GRACE

Ummm, I forgot how good you always smell. Remind me one more time.

> *They kiss a little longer this time. Grace looks around her to see the table beautifully set with fresh flowers/roses, her favorite, everywhere.*

GRACE (CONT'D)

Something smells incredible! Where's Tucker?

MITCH

I told him if he outdid himself with dinner that he could take the rest of the evening off.

                    GRACE

Aahhh... So we're alone are we?

                    MITCH

You're not going to try to take advantage of me,
are you?

                    GRACE

              (blushing)

It depends on how good dinner is.

              (laughing)

                         Mitch hands Grace a glass of
                         wine

                    MITCH

Well, we're about to find out.

                         Mitch seats Grace at the
                         table and brings out two
                         plates.

                    MITCH (CONT'D)

Shall we?

                         They start eating and
                         CHATTING lightly throughout
                         the meal.

                    GRACE

Mmmm.... It tastes even better than it smells.
Thank you for such a lovely dinner, Mitch. You
always go out of your way to make me feel
special and I probably don't deserve it most of
the time. I know I get all wrapped up in my
life, myself.... Why do you put up with me?

                    MITCH

Well, because I love you, I guess. But... I
will admit, that I do make more of a concerted
effort to think about us and I think it's time
that you did too!

                    GRACE

Mitch,

          (taking his hand)

I do love you.

                         They finish eating and Mitch
                         brings out a glass of Brandy
                         for the two of them and takes
                         her hand as she rises from
                         the table. Grace slowly sips
                         her Brandy.

               GRACE (CONT'D)

Is this desert?

MITCH

Well, I was hoping that you might be.

They embrace and start kissing.

GRACE

I forgot how incredible you are.

(running her hands over his body)

MITCH

I'm never going to let you forget again.

FADE OUT/CUT TO

III.10 INT - LIVING ROOM - LATE EVENING

Grace and Mitch are sleeping on the couch, wrapped up in a big blanket. The sound of heavy rain wakens them.

GRACE

It's raining? God, I don't remember the last time it rained!

Mitch's phone RINGS and he answers, half asleep.

MITCH

Yes, this is Mitch Haverhill. Bob, slow down, yes, she is here

> (his voice rises, and he is visibly shaken)

What... Oh my God...

Grace, It's Gabrielle!

GRACE

> (terror in her face and her voice is trembling)

What about her? Where is she? Oh God...

> (jumping up and throwing on the first clothes she finds)

Is she OK? What is it? Damn it, Mitch, what is it?

MITCH

> (still talking into the phone to the Police Chief)

Where? OK, Bob, we'll be right there! Yeah, about ten minutes.

> (hangs up the phone with terror in his eyes, visibly shaken)

She's been in an accident, Grace, she's badly hurt, let's go!

*Tears are streaming down
Grace's face. As they exit,
she throws her hair in a
ponytail. Grace is getting
hysterical.*

FADE OUT/CUT TO:

ACT IV

TRAGEDY

IV.1 EXT. - ACCIDENT SCENE - LATE EVENING

> *The stage is dark and Grace
> and Mitch can be heard in the
> background, in a frantic,
> terrified conversation as
> they make their way to the
> accident scene.*

GRACE

Where is she? Where is she?

MITCH

Not far from here!

GRACE

Hurry, we must hurry, oh please, Mitch... Did
another car hit her? She's alright Mitch? Tell
me she's alright...

(screaming)

Tell me she's alright!

                    MITCH

I don't know all of the details, let's just get
there!

                    GRACE

Oh God, we had a nice conversation this morning,
but I haven't seen her since I accused her of
embarrassing me last weekend! I need to
apologize! Oh God, please let her be OK, so
that I can apologize!

                    The sound of
                    THUNDER/LIGHTENING continues.

                                    CUT TO:

IV.2 EXT. ACCIDENT SCENE - LATE EVENING

                    The stage is dark with a
                    spotlight on a blanket-
                    covered figure.

                    Grace is now SCREAMING and
                    hysterical.

                    GRACE

Where is she? Please someone, where is she?

                    Grace runs over to the
                    blanket. She is now truly
                    SCREAMING and hysterical.

GRACE (CONT'D)

Gabe... Where, Gabrielle......?

> *She sees that it must be her*
> *sister. Mitch is trying to*
> *keep her away from the*
> *gruesome scene. Grace falls*
> *to the ground and cradles her*
> *sister's bleeding head ...*
> *She is dead.*

GRACE (CONT'D)

Gabe?... Sweetheart, it's OK, it's me, Grace and
I'm here with you now. I'll keep you warm until
we can get you to the hospital and get you all
stitched up. Wake up, Gabe! Mitch is here too!
Everything is going to be OK!

> *Mitch has tears streaming*
> *down his face. He tries to*
> *pull Grace away.*

MITCH

Grace, she's gone, she's gone, oh God, she's
gone!

> *He sits down on the ground*
> *and SOBS violently!*

GRACE

She can't be, no, no... she can't be.

> (staring at her sister in
> disbelief)

*She gets up stumbling, dazed
and in shock. She is soaking
wet, covered in her sister's
blood and hysterical.
Shaking her fists in the air
as if to bring down the
heavens!*

GRACE (CONT'D)

(screaming)

Who am I going to take care of now? Who am I
going to take care of now?

*She falls to the ground on
her knees, SOBBING.*

CUT TO:

IV.3 INT. - THE RED ROOM - SAME TIME

*The stage is dark with a
spotlight on Benjamin
Franklin sitting alone. There
is a single tear streaming
down his cheek. George
Washington enters the room
and gently places a hand on
Franklin's shoulder.*

GEORGE WASHINGTON

Have faith, dear Benjamin, as sometimes the good
Lord knows what is best and has other plans for
us in the here and after.

BENJAMIN FRANKLIN

Aahh... George, my friend, what purpose can the
tears of an old man serve?

GEORGE WASHINGTON

Do not underestimate the salt of your tears, my
friend.

BENJAMIN FRANKLIN

I have been blessed to live to an age of wisdom
and maturity. It is difficult to witness the
taking of one so young and promising.

GEORGE WASHINGTON

When a young life is ended, we must
wholeheartedly trust in the fact that there is
greater work for them to be doing elsewhere!

(looking up to the Heavens)

Her journey has just started. From your infancy
you have loved **JUSTICE, LIBERTY** and **CONCORD**, in
a way that has made it natural and consistent
for you to live your life as an example of your
virtues.

BENJAMIN FRANKLIN

Thank you, my dear friend. You speak words of
great comfort to thine old ears. As constant
good fortune has accompanied me even to an
advanced period of life and when I reflect on
it, which is frequently the case, I am inclined

to say that were it left to my choice I should
have no objection to go over the same life from
its beginning to the end; only asking the
advantage...of correcting in a second edition
some faults of the first.

GEORGE WASHINGTON

I see no faults in you man... I see only your
virtues!

BENJAMIN FRANKLIN

But on the whole, though I never arrived at the
perfection I had been so ambitious of obtaining,
but fell far short of it, yet I was, by the
endeavor, a better and happier man than I
otherwise should have been if I had not
attempted it.

GEORGE WASHINGTON

You are a shining example of humility, sincerity
and good will towards men. Why Benjamin, your
life has been an incredible journey of knowledge
applied to life and efforts leading to
accomplishments!

(pauses for effect)

Why Benjamin, let me recount just some of the
multitude of personal contributions that this
young country has had the advantage of enjoying
as for the likes of you: your pioneering
efforts in that of the print shop, your
successful newspaper, "The Pennsylvania
Gazette," the first subscription libraries, the

first public hospital facility in the city of
Philadelphia, your contributions as a founder of
the University of Philadelphia, your tenure as
Postmaster General, the driving force behind the
first fire companies, the lightening rod

> (spoken with great enthusiasm,
>   pomp, respect and excitability,
>   as the list grows on)

Dual-purpose spectacles, your ingenious, fuel-
efficient wood burning stove... And did I
mention electricity? Why no, and what about the
consistent and reliable words of wisdom and
anecdotes we have all come to know and love
because of Poor Richards Almanac! Your
incredible contributions in your later years, as
a great statesman and negotiator between our
country and both France and England!

BENJAMIN FRANKLIN

Oh George, you certainly do me well! I have
always thought that one man of tolerable
abilities may work great changes and accomplish
great affairs among mankind if he first forms a
good plan, and cutting off all amusements or
other employments that would divert his
attention, makes the execution of that same plan
his sole study and business.

> (pauses for effect)

I had therefore a tolerable character to begin
in the world with. I valued it properly and
determined to preserve it. I grew convinced
that truth, sincerity and integrity, in dealings
between man and man, were of the utmost
importance in the felicity of life. I listen

upon some of the bickerings back and forth
between opposing counsels we currently witness
in presenting their arguments and I am baffled
by their ignorance as to the art of conversation
and hence, negotiation.

GEORGE WASHINGTON

Quite right, Benjamin, quite right! Go on man,
as always, I never tire of your observations!

BENJAMIN FRANKLIN

As the chief ends of conversation are to inform,
or to be informed, to please or to persuade, I
wish well-meaning and sensible men would not
lessen their power of doing good by a positive,
assuming manner that seldom fails to disgust,
tends to create opposition, and to defeat every
one of those purposes for which speech was given
to us. This Lester is no gentlemen, why he is
the scourge of the earth! We must love our
fellow man and teach others to do the same by
our conduct!

> *Thomas Jefferson quietly*
> *walks in and joins the two*
> *men. He puts his hand on*
> *Franklin's shoulder.*

THOMAS JEFFERSON

Of course you raise issues of great salience,
Benjamin! Style in writing or speaking is formed
very early in life, while the imagination is
warm, and impressions are permanent.

                    (pauses for effect)

This hatred and intolerance must be getting
handed down from father to son.

                    (pauses for effect)

Whenever you are to do a thing, though it can
never be known but to yourself, ask yourself how
you would act were the whole world looking at
you, and act accordingly. I... never believed
there was one code of morality for a public
[man], and another for a private man. The moral
sense is as much a part of our constitution as
that of feeling, seeing, or hearing. It is not
enough to speak,

                    (pauses for effect)

But to speak true. For things are often spoke
and seldom meant. **WORDS MATTER**!

                    BENJAMIN FRANKLIN

Keep conscience clear. Then never fear. Use no
hurtful deceit; think innocently and justly and,
if you speak, speak accordingly. We may give
advice but we cannot give conduct.

                    GEORGE WASHINGTON

Your years have proven you to be more sage and
possessing of wisdom than any of the finest
beings I could boast to know, Benjamin.

                    BENJAMIN FRANKLIN

Respect and reason wait on wrinkled age.

>   (pauses for effect)

These disputing, contradicting, and confuting
people are generally unfortunate in their
affairs. They get victory sometimes, but they
never get good will, which would be of more use
to them.

>   (pauses for effect)

I grow old and tired, but nonetheless was
content to spend the rest of my days, amongst
the greatness of the likes of you, my dear
friend and fearless leader.

>   GEORGE WASHINGTON

I have no other view than to promote the public
good and am unambitious of honors not founded in
the approbation of my Country.

>   BENJAMIN FRANKLIN

To serve the public faithfully, and at the same
time please it entirely, is impracticable.

>   (pauses for effect and said with
>   great conviction)

**Why George, hide not your talents, they for use
were made. What's a sundial in the shade!**

>   (Said with great theatrical pomp
>   and circumstance)

George Washington, Commander of the American
armies, who, like Joshua of old, commanded the
sun and the moon to stand still, and they obeyed
him. Here you would know and enjoy what

posterity will say on Washington. For a
thousand leagues have nearly the same effect
with a thousand years.

> *Hands George Washington his*
> *crab-tree walking stick,*
> *symbolically to assist him on*
> *his stroll to immortality.*

BENJAMIN FRANKLIN (CONT'D)

To the man who unites all hearts. If it were a
scepter, [thee] has merited it and would become
it.

> *Benjamin Franklin exits the*
> *stage ceremoniously and*
> *dignified.*

GEORGE WASHINGTON

He snatched the lightening from the sky and the
scepter from tyrants.

> *Thomas Jefferson walks over*
> *to George Washington and*
> *places a hand on his*
> *shoulder.*

THOMAS JEFFERSON

He was the greatest man and ornament of the age
and country in which he lived.

CUT TO:

IV.4 INT. HELEN'S BEACH HOUSE - AFTERNOON

> *Grace enters and it looks
> like she hasn't slept or
> showered in days. She
> practically falls into
> Helen's arms, hysterical.*

GRACE

(sobbing)

Helen! Thank you for letting me come over on
such short notice.

> *The two warmly embrace.*

HELEN

(speaking with deep concern)

You know I'm only a phone call away, Grace. I
know, my dear, my heart is breaking too!

GRACE

(through sobs)

She was all I had left and I judged her too
harshly! Who am I to judge? She was my little
sister not a criminal, not one of my cases. She
was right, I never knew when to turn it off...to
call it a day.

> *SOBBING hysterically*

HELEN

Stop it, Grace! You cannot hold yourself
responsible for acts of God! You loved her and
you were concerned for her well-being. That's
what big sisters do!

GRACE

I could have been...should have been, more
understanding! I could have been more of a
friend, versus her biggest critic!

HELEN

Grace, your only crime was caring. And, do I
really need to point out to you how wonderful of
a friend you always were to her? Why some of my
earliest memories are the two of you, walking
arm in arm down to the end of the dock, giggling
and doing silly, little girl things, as you sat
and fed the seagulls. She knows how much you
cared.

GRACE

But, but...the last time we were together was
awful. I accused her of embarrassing me and she
left.

HELEN

Knowing Gabe, she probably did embarrass you!
She had to blaze her own trail, Grace...you
couldn't stop her and that was one of her
attributes that I will always admire! She
followed her heart!

GRACE

And what is it that I follow, Helen? A legacy?

(sobbing violently)

I am alone....I am all alone...

HELEN

(hugging her with deep concern)

No, my dear, though it may seem so now, you are
far from alone. Stu and I will always be here
for you, with open arms, like loving parents.
But, most importantly, you have Mitch. Now is
the time to reach out to him.

GRACE

I don't know, Helen. He is wonderful and I do
love him. But I am concerned that our
differences will only lead to heartbreak down the
road.

HELEN

Differences? The only time differences matter
is if your values are different too. You and
Mitch are so much alike in more ways than you
care to admit and I know that if you were to be
honest with yourself, you would agree.

GRACE

He is special in so many ways! I am not sure
that I deserve or want such devotion.

HELEN

Don't want? Grace, it's time to tear down that
wall! You want and you want deeply! Your law
books won't keep you warm for the rest of your
life...but Mitch will. I fear you will lose him
too, if you don't take a good hard look at the
situation and realize your destiny.

GRACE

Will she ever forgive me, Helen?

HELEN

She already has. And she will be smiling down
at you from the heavens...when you start to
follow YOUR heart! One of the hardest lessons
to learn is that some of the most important
actors in our lives don't stick around for the
final curtain call. Take all of the wonderful
lessons she taught you about life and let them
help you to live the rest of yours.

GRACE

Thank you, Helen!

(the two hug again)

HELEN

I know you will do the right thing. Let **PROVIDENCE** be
your guide and everything else will fall into place.

The two hug and both exit.

CUT TO:

ACT V

TRIUMPH

V.1 INT. THE COURTROOM - MORNING

> *Grace enters the courtroom.*

BAILIFF

All rise, the Honorable Grace Porter presiding.

> *Grace takes her seat and POUNDS the gavel.*

GRACE

Please be seated. Court is now in session. Counselors, are you prepared to give closing statements?

> *Snayder and Pantovere stand in unison.*

SNAYDER/PANTOVERE

We are your Honor.

> (spoken in unison, as well)

SNAYDER

Your Honor, ladies and gentlemen of the jury, I believe this court has witnessed enough

plausible testimony and evidence to raise
questionable doubt as to the guilt of my client,
Noah Lester, on the charges of aiding and
abetting in the murder of The Walker family and
in conspiracy to commit a felony.

(he pauses for a moment)

No one can underestimate the loss of Mr. Walker
and his family. No one can understand their
grief or their pain, but as citizens of the
United States, we can all certainly understand
their desire for the guilty to be held
accountable for the heinous acts committed, but
that is my point here today, ladies and
gentleman of the jury, JUSTICE HAS ALREADY BEEN
SERVED! Alan Shields was convicted and
sentenced with first degree murder and numerous
other felonies and is awaiting sentencing for
additional charges. You heard testimony from
another member of Mr. Lester's society that was
given the same instructions and chose not to
follow those same instructions!

(pauses for effect)

It isn't Mr. Lester's instructions that are at
issue here, it is Mr. Shield's response to them!

THIS HAS GONE TOO FAR! Noah Lester's life has
been turned upside down by the allegations made
on his behalf in this courtroom...

(pauses for effect)

And HE WANTS HIS LIFE BACK NOW!

> *SLAMMING his fists on the
> desk!*

The fate of Noah Lester rests in your hands. It
is the government and the law making bodies that
comprise the judicial system OF THIS COUNTRY
that threaten you and THIS GREAT COUNTRY by
allowing for an overly narrow or "strict"
interpretation of the Constitution and The Bill
of Rights meant to protect us. You as members of
the jury and citizens of this country will be
sending a dangerous message that our most
fundamental rights and liberties are invalid in
this court of law, if you allow for anything but
a verdict of not guilty. The Due Process Clause
protects the accused against conviction except
upon proof beyond a reasonable doubt of every
fact necessary to constitute the crime with
which he is charged.

(pauses for effect)

If you cannot convict my client without a
reasonable doubt, you must find him innocent of
all charges against him. Thank you ladies and
gentlemen of the jury. I have nothing further,
your Honor. The defense rests.

PANTOVERE

Your Honor, ladies and gentlemen of the jury,
thank you for your patience and your undivided
attention during these court proceedings. You
have seen footage of the actual act of domestic
terrorism, in which Alan Shields drove his car
into the Walker family and other peaceful
protesters during the Charlottesville rally.
You have read and listened to the hate-filled
preparations for the rally and the violence-
inducing instructions shared on Discord and
other social media platforms. You saw Mr.
Lester's communications to Mr. Shields, keeping

him informed as to the Walker family's
whereabouts and pinpointing their location for
the mass carnage.

(pauses for effect)

Ladies and gentlemen of the jury, how can you
not return anything but a verdict of guilty in
these proceedings against Noah Lester? Defense
counsel has repeatedly used far-fetched
interpretations of inapplicable precedence
rulings and has drawn inapplicable parallels to
confuse us into believing Mr. Lester's
innocence. Alan Shields has already provided
testimony to law enforcement regarding the plot
that he and Mr. Lester devised to target and
terrorize the Walker family, all but
guaranteeing their demise! Even if Mr. Shields
had not been found guilty, Mr. Lester can still
be found guilty of aiding and abetting, please
keep that in mind.

SNAYDER

Objection, your Honor! Counsel is leading the
jury!

GRACE

Sustained! Proceed with caution, Mr. Pantovere!

PANTOVERE

Of course, your Honor. First Amendment
protection is not a defense in a charge of
aiding and abetting in a murder charge or in the
charge of conspiracy to commit a felony. All

over the past two hundred years and more, we, as
Americans, have proven this nomenclature to
signify the most unified, peace-loving and
progressive citizenry in the world. I am not
proud to call you an "American," Mr. Lester, and
neither was former Virginia Governor, Terry
McAuliffe, who after the devastation at
Charlottesville said, "Let's be honest, they
need to leave America, because they are not
Americans." I fear you have no conscience, Mr.
Lester.

(pauses for effect)

When I read and hear the dogma and propaganda
you speak as the gospel to your followers, you
must accept the fact that you attempt to set us
back to the 1950s and 1960s, why as far back as
the 1860s and earlier. Throughout these decades
there have always been fringe groups like yours
rearing their ugly heads but democracy wins,
equality and love for our brother man, wins!
Looking back to 1896, Justice John Marshall
Harlan wrote the only dissenting opinion in
Plessy v. Ferguson and stated, "The Constitution
is colorblind, and neither knows nor tolerates
classes among citizens."

(pauses for effect and spoken with
great disdain)

I have never heard the phrase, "kiked-up, nigger
experiment." Where do those words come from,
Mr. Lester? They are not in my vocabulary, not
on dictionary.com. **I DO NOT KNOW THOSE WORDS!**

*SLAMMING her fists on the
desk*

Hate is an insidious disease that gets passed
down from generation to generation. It is a
learned emotion and reaction to people and
ideals that differ from you and yours. To quote
the late Dr. Martin Luther King, Jr., "Morality
cannot be legislated, but behavior can be
regulated. Judicial decrees may not change the
heart, but they can restrain the heartless." Do
you have children, Mr. Lester?

                    NOAH LESTER

Yes, two.

                    GRACE

And are you teaching them to pass on your hate-
filled ideologies?

                    NOAH LESTER

You choose words that reflect your opinion of
the subject matter at hand. I do not happen to
agree with your opinion.

                    GRACE

Lose your indignation, Mr. Lester. I am saying
to all of you present in this courtroom today,
THAT THIS IS WHERE IT MUST STOP! You, Mr.
Lester, are a hypocrite! We live in the
greatest country in the world. We have freedoms
and luxuries that cannot be attained most
anywhere else and there are people living in
this world who would do anything to have the
chance to live in The United States of America,
the oldest enduring republic in world history.

I repeat, we are a country of great freedoms!
The public and I quote, Mr. Lester, "has grown
weary of seeing the First Amendment dragged out
as the savior of the unsavory set." It is time
that we as individuals stand up and take
responsibility. What made you think that you
could incite and encourage another human being
to kill and injure other human beings and then
hide behind the First Amendment? It's like that
old saying, It's easier to ask for forgiveness
than ask for permission, isn't that right, Mr.
Lester?

> *There is a hush in the*
> *courtroom and Noah Lester*
> *hesitates to answer the*
> *judge's question.*

GRACE (CONT'D)

Your response, Mr. Lester, I am losing my
patience!

NOAH LESTER

I feel we all have the right to speak and share
our opinions and viewpoints that bring value to
our cause or help to move our cause forward.
Alan Shields was the driver of the car, not me!

GRACE

When you point the finger of blame at someone
else, there are three fingers pointing back at
yourself, Mr. Lester!

*Grace points her finger at
Noah Lester and turns the
side of her hand to the jury
and courtroom to emphasize
her point.*

Your very specific instructions were a direct
incitement to violence that led to the deaths,
no the murders, of Susan Leiberman Walker and
Hope Walker and Bryant Walker. You are just as
guilty as the driver of the vehicle! You have
scarred Tyrone Walker and his family in a way
that will never heal. I take a stand today, to
let you know that both as an officer of the
court of the Commonwealth of Virginia and as a
member of the judiciary branch of the federal
government, I am willing to stand up and say, **WE
HAVE HAD ENOUGH!**

> (she pauses and you can hear
> affirmation of purpose in her
> voice)

You have been found guilty of aiding and
abetting in the murder of Susan Leiberman
Walker, Hope Walker and Bryant Walker and in
conspiracy to commit a felony, Mr. Lester, and
let me make an UNPRECEDENTED sentence on your
behalf of forty years to life in a maximum
security, federal prison, with no eligibility
for parole until after year twenty, a $100,000
fine payable within sixty days of sentencing and
to include 1000 hours of community service at
the discretion of the penal institution and bi-
weekly psychiatric counseling, again, at the
discretion of the penal institution.

> (pauses for effect)

Let this send a message to others in your white
supremacist groups that murdering innocent
protesters and terrorizing peaceful communities
in the name of fascism or neo-nazism or any
other group, espousing white nationalist hate-
filled rhetoric, that your time is up! Your days
are numbered! As it has been said before,
"Revolutions don't move backwards." You and
your white supremacist fringe groups are never
welcome again in Charlottesville, VA or any
other city in our **VERY FINE** country!

> (pauses for effect)

I am proud to call myself "American" and I want
everyone in this courtroom today to leave here
proud, too!

> (she starts to gather her papers,
> as she continues to speak
> passionately)

The Bill of Rights, as written by our founding
fathers, was meant to protect minorities from
persecution, not deviants from getting their
just deserves. From the start of this trial, I
have listened to counsel on both sides quoting
the guys who wrote the stuff, sometimes
passionately and sometimes reprehensibly, so in
adjourning, I shall follow suit, but do so,
respectfully. Alexander Hamilton once said,
"**JUSTICE** is the end of government. It is the
end of civil society. It has ever been and ever
will be pursued until it be obtained, or until
LIBERTY be lost in the pursuit."

> (pauses for effect)

Over two hundred years ago, our founding fathers
set out to draft and institute an ideology of

both a body of laws to govern by and an undeniable set of liberties and freedoms to emancipate and protect the sovereign interests of this great country. While it hasn't been perfect, it remains a framework that has stood the test of time, civil disobedience, world wars, racial desegregation and ongoing systemic racism, religious intolerance, terrorism and a myriad of other adversities; but in my courtroom, **JUSTICE** will prevail!

> (pauses for effect)

Let this day serve as an example to you and anyone who aspires to your ill advised exploitations of The Bill of Rights and more specifically, the First Amendment. **JUSTICE** is truth in action and **JUSTICE** has been served! Court is adjourned.

> *Grace POUNDS the gavel and stands to exit.*

> CUT TO:

V.8 INT. FLASHBACK - THE RED ROOM - SAME TIME

> *Show all of the founding fathers, except for Franklin, cheering with unanimous applause and patting each other on the backs in response to the courageous judge and her fiery sentence.*

> CUT TO:

V.9 INT. BACK AT THE COURTROOM - SAME TIME

> *There is great applause in
> the courtroom and much
> excitement as the judge
> stands and makes her exit.*
>
> *Snayder is trying to calm his
> client and is assuring him
> that he will appeal on his
> behalf.*
>
> *In the background, dub in the
> voices of a group of children
> reciting "The Pledge of
> Allegiance"*

> CUT TO:

V.10 EXT. - LATER

> *We witness a casual, lovely
> setting, with Grace and
> Mitch, obviously just wed and
> mingling among a small group
> of guests.*
>
> *There is applause as they
> kiss and the story ends.*

> THE CURTAIN FALLS AND
> RISES AGAIN AFTER
> A BRIEF PAUSE

> *To music: Gabrielle, in an
> angelic-looking costume, with
> a faint halo over her head,
> dances to the music and with
> each of the cast, as they*

take their bows, especially
flirtatious with Benjamin
Franklin and A.J.

THE CURTAIN FALLS

Made in the USA
Columbia, SC
09 February 2021